ravenwood

MADALYN RAE

book content warning

I am not one to issue trigger warnings; however, I feel this book might warrant a few. Please be aware of the following contents.

- Mentions of trafficking and sex crimes
- Mentions of being drugged for sexual reasons

ravenwood university

THE DRESS FRAN insisted I wear is too tight and getting on my nerves. "Quit squirming," Fran reprimands from the driver's seat. "You're going to wrinkle that skirt, and it was a bitch to iron."

"This is college. Most students are going to be wearing leggings and a sweatshirt. Why did you insist on me wearing a semiformal dress?"

"You only get one chance to make a first impression," Fran reminds me for the hundredth time.

"It's the twenty-first century. No one cares about first impressions anymore. College is supposed to be a time for me to discover who I am. A time to let loose and be free while smoking marijuana and having random sex with strangers I meet in a bar, using my fake ID." I cross my arms across my chest. "Not to worry about first impressions with people who won't remember my name in five years."

"You're acting like a teenager."

"Theoretically, I am a teenager," I retort.

Fran laughs as we pass under the stone archway, welcoming us to *Ravenwood University*. The narrow road is lined with ancient live oak trees that reach across the top of the road, joining their long branches to form a hidden driveway. We enter the school grounds, and the beauty of the campus takes my breath away.

Unlike a traditional university that covers several blocks or more, Ravenwood's entire school is housed in four buildings. The main building, sitting at the end of the circular drive, is straight out of a *Harry Potter* book. It looks more like a castle than a university.

"How much is this place costing me?" I ask, sliding out of the seat.

"Enough," Fran answers. She meets me at the back of the SUV, and together, we unload the three suitcases I packed most of my belongings in.

"Remind me again why I wanted to do this." We walk toward the front door of the main building. Around me, students are milling about, greeting each other with warm hugs and laughs.

"Because you wanted the life experience of a college student." She shakes her head dramatically, pretending to mimic me.

"I'm thinking that was dumb." We enter the front door to a large open room full of tables and people surrounding them.

"Welcome to Freshman move-in day!" an overly chipper older woman says. "We're so glad you've chosen Ravenwood!" She sounds like she's repeated the same speech several times today.

"Thank you." I smile. "I'm happy to be here."

"I'm Tori Stewart, your guidance counselor." She sticks her hand in front of me, and I half-heartedly shake it. "Check in at that table over there, and they'll let you know your room number." She points toward the other side of the room.

We move to the shortest line and wait with everyone else. It's not until we've been in line for at least ten minutes that I notice we're standing in the N-Z section. "We're in the wrong line, Fran," I whisper.

"Well, shit." We slide over to the A-M line, which is twice as long. Thankfully, the line moves quickly, and the young woman at the table greets us with a smile.

"Name, please."

"Celeste Luquire."

She sifts through the L's, finding my card quickly. "You're in room 246." The girl shares a look with the girl next to her, piquing my curiosity. "Here is your room and building key. Make sure you keep it with you at all times. Did you get your schedule?"

"Yes. It was emailed to me last week."

The girl smiles. "Then you're good to go. If you have any questions, your RA will be in the room closest to the stairwell."

Exiting the main building, we cross the traffic circle and enter a building that's similar in architecture, but much smaller than the main building. Just as the girl said, my card opens the dorm door, straight into an older stairwell. "What room did she say?" Fran asks, dragging a suitcase behind her.

"246." We exit the stairs, and I find the RA's room quickly, making a mental note of its whereabouts. We pass every room on the floor until we make it to the end of the hallway and the door with the correct number on it.

"Finally," Fran says, setting the suitcases on the wooden floor.

"Should I knock or just go in?" For some reason, I'm nervous. I don't have a chance to do either. The door cracks open, and a voice mumbles through the narrow opening.

"Why are you standing outside my door?"

"Umm, hi. My name is Celeste. I think I'm your roommate."

"Yeeeaaah," the door opener's voice is laced with sarcasm. I don't know whether to laugh or cry. She opens the door fully, giving us a full view of the room that will be my home for the next nine months.

"This is your side," my roommate announces as if it wasn't obvious. The room has two twin-size beds plastered against the sides of the room, with built-in desks and closets at the foot of each. Her side looks to have been decorated by Satan himself. Solid black bedding, complete with black flowered pillows and décor, covers the top of her mattress. A thick black carpet sits underneath the bed, giving her side the extra splash of Goth she needs. A skull sits in the middle of her desk, with a black candle sticking out of the top, completing the look.

"Oh, my. Can you burn candles in dorm rooms? I remember reading something about that being against the rules." Fran moves away from the girl.

"It may be. Who knows? Maybe if I burn this place down, then I would be free of this shithole." She jumps back on her bed, turning her back to the two of us.

Fran opens her eyes wide. I shake my head, agreeing with her silent question. She turns and begins unpacking my bags.

"I'll do this. You have a long drive home." I set my hand on top of hers.

"Are you sure?"

"Yes, ma'am." I smile and wrap my arms around my caregiver. "It'll give me time to get to know my new roommate." I hear a deep sigh behind me, making me smile.

Fran pulls me tight. "Keep in touch." She pulls away, wiping a tear from her cheek. "I'm going to miss you."

"I'm going to miss you, too. I promise to call you every week."

Fran sniffs. "You better."

"I'll walk you back to the car." I grab my keycard and follow the older woman back outside.

"It's not too late to change your mind," Fran says as we reach the driver's door.

"I know. This is something I need to do on my own. Something I *want* to do."

"You already have three doctoral degrees. What's the point in earning a bachelor's degree in general studies?"

"It's not about the degree. It's about the life experience. Besides, these people don't know I have a triple doctorate. They'll think I'm like them." I smile, hoping to reassure her.

Fran nods, sliding a loose strand of hair behind my ear. "I understand, even if I'm not happy about it. If you need anything, please let me know."

"I will." I open the door, helping her inside. She slides behind the wheel and wipes another tear.

I give her one last hug before closing her safely inside. "I love you."

"I love you, too."

"Now, go home. I'm going to be okay."

Fran starts the car and fastens her seat belt. "I'm not happy about this." She blows me a kiss before driving away, making me second-guess the only decision I've ever made for myself.

Is this what I need to do? I take a deep breath and answer my own question. Yes, it is.

Heading back to the second-floor dorm, I scan my card, and the room door pops open. "You're back." My roommate's voice is flat and monotone.

"I am. You sound excited."

She shrugs. "Eh. My name's Emeryn."

"Celeste," I answer. "Emeryn is a beautiful name. I don't think I've ever heard it before.

"Yeah, my mom was into all that new age shit when she was pregnant. It makes it hard to find a keychain with your name printed on it, though. Where are you from?"

"New Orleans. You?"

"Jackson, Mississippi."

"That's not too far. Our commute was a little longer." I suck at normal conversation. Instead of making a fool out of myself, I decide to unpack my bags and fill the small chest of drawers with my clothes.

"Was that your mom?" Emeryn asks from her side of the room.

My mother is dead. I killed her. Somehow, that doesn't feel like the best response. I choose a less controversial answer. "Yes."

"What about your father?" Emeryn is nosey.

"He's dead." I don't let my mind think about the last minutes with him or the way he died. Those memories are hidden safely in my mind.

She scoffs. "Mine, too. It's not a big loss, though. He was an ass." I don't respond because I can't relate. My father, Viktor, could be an ass, but he cherished the ground I walked on. "Hungry?" she asks, interrupting my dark thoughts. "It's about time for dinner."

"No, I'm good. I need to unpack and get my side set up. Thank you for the invitation."

"Suit yourself. I'm going to eat. Don't steal any of my shit while I'm gone," Emeryn warns as she exits the room. I laugh, hoping that she's joking. Something tells me she's not.

Unpacking my bedding, I can't help but compare it to the stark black version on the opposite side of the room. Fran picked out a soft pink comforter with bright white flowers accenting the Egyptian cotton sheets that match perfectly. Emeryn's side says Bad Girl, while mine says Ruffles and Lace. "This is what you wanted," I remind myself as the butterflies take flight in my stomach.

A few hours pass before my side of the room is in full froufrou mode, leaving me with nothing to do. I head back to the main building, where several students are still wandering around, talking to the remaining people behind the tables.

I stop at the first table I pass. A beautiful girl greets me. "Hello!"

"Hi."

"Would you like information about the chess club?"

"Is that what this is?"

She smiles. "It is. I hoped the huge chessboard attached to the front of the table would give a clue, but alas, I was wrong."

I laugh, stepping back and seeing the obvious board in front of me. "You're right. I think it needs to be bigger."

"I'm sorry. I don't mean to sound sarcastic. My name is Darby." She sticks her hand out to shake mine. "I'm a chess nerd."

"Celeste," I answer. "I am not a chess nerd, but I appreciate the game."

"Understood. I'll wait here for my next victim. Maybe I'll see you around."

"Sure." I step away, scanning the tables, looking for something interesting. I smile the moment I see it. A hastily drawn "Coding Club" sign grabs my attention.

"Hi," the guy behind the table greets me. "Are you interested in coding?"

"Kind of." I smile.

"Do you know anything about it?"

"Coding? Some." My third doctoral degree is in computer science, and I've written code for many large companies. I don't share that with him.

He hands me a brochure. Instead of the normal font of an informational brochure, everything is written in code. "All of our information is on here. We'd love to have you join us."

I look over the brochure, searching for a meeting place and time. There is nothing but a long string of ones and zeros. "I'm guessing I need to translate this to figure out when and where."

He smiles, flashing white teeth and dimples. "I

didn't design that, but yes, that's the plan." He looks around and whispers. "I can tell you if that would be easier."

I return the smile. "No. I'll figure it out." I relish the challenge, even though there's not much of a challenge here.

"Drake." He holds his hand toward me.

"Celeste." I touch his hand, and the moment our hands touch, something passes between us. He feels it too. He pulls his hand away as quickly as he sent it.

Drake clears his throat. "I think I shocked you. Static electricity can be a bitch. I hope you can join us."

"I'd like that." I pull the brochure back in front of my face, reading the binary code without the use of my computer. "See you Wednesday at six-thirty." I smile, turn, and feel his eyes on me until I exit the building.

My phone buzzes in my pocket. I pull it out to find a text from Fran, telling me she made it home safely, along with another text from an unknown number that makes my heart jump into my throat.

Remember the rules.

I don't respond and slide my phone back into its resting place. "How could I forget the rules? You're not going to let me," I mumble, working my way back to the dorm.

Thankfully, Emeryn hasn't returned. My stomach growls, reminding me that it's been a few days since

I've eaten. I pull a bottle of goat blood from my back-pack and drink it in one gulp. It hits every taste bud, quenching my monstrous hunger instantly.

"Did you just drink...blood?" My roommate is standing in the doorframe, staring at the small stain remaining on my shirt.

the first day

EMERYN and I stare at each other longer than necessary. I slowly screw the lid back on the glass bottle and set it on my desk.

"Blood? No, that's gross. This is tomato juice. I'm on a special diet."

She comes fully into the room, closing the door behind her. "You sure? That looks like blood to me. It's too thick to be tomato juice. Wrong color, too."

"Positive. My...my mother grows special tomatoes in her garden. They are full of vitamins and minerals that she's harvested throughout the year." I pat my stomach, hoping to stop her line of questioning.

"Whatever." Emeryn throws herself on top of her bed and sticks her earbuds in. That's the universal sign for "*leave me alone.*"

I do just that and pretend to work on my side of the room. I pull my schedule out, looking through the list of freshman-level courses. I dread the simplicity of the work but relish the opportunity to be normal. Something I've never been in the nearly eight hundred years I've walked this planet.

Emeryn falls asleep close to midnight. Her breathing has slowed, along with her heart rate. I stretch my stiff muscles, which have been tense from pretending to be asleep for the past few hours. Pulling out Drake's brochure from earlier, I open my laptop and enter the code exactly as it's written on the brochure. Most of it I'm able to read on my own, but one part has kept me guessing since earlier. I laugh when the words come across my computer screen.

If you've figured out how to read this, you're in. If you can't read this, then you never will, so never mind.

Very poetic, guys.

The sun begins rising over the horizon, sending bright light into the room. I close my laptop after hours of researching anything I could think to research and resume my ruse of sleeping. My alarm sounds on my phone minutes later, "waking" me.

I take my time getting dressed, pulling my bright red curls into a high ponytail, and slide into a pair of skinny jeans. My father preferred me to dress in clothes from times past. Since his passing, I've moved up a couple of centuries and ventured into skinny jeans and leggings. I slide on a pair of knee-high boots and a turquoise cropped sweater, along with a pair of earrings that are the perfect match to the sweater, just as Emeryn wakes for the morning.

"You're up early."

"I guess I'm hungry this morning." I smile.

"Don't you need more of your *tomato* juice?"

"Nope. I only drink that at night." I sling my backpack over my shoulder. "See you later. Maybe we'll have some classes together."

"I doubt it," she mumbles from bed as I close the door behind me. Emeryn is making it hard to like her, but I refuse to give up.

I take the stairs two at a time and head across the circular drive to the mess hall. I don't eat human food, but if I want the full experience of college life, I need to pretend. I'm taking the opportunity to participate in everything I can. Everything that's been denied my entire life.

A few students are scattered throughout the large room. It's early, and most are most likely still sleeping. I grab a tray and head through the line. "Hello there," an older woman greets me with a smile. "You're the first freshman I've had the pleasure of seeing this morning."

"Really? I'm Celeste."

"Well then, welcome, Celeste. What would you like to eat on this fine day?"

I look at the massive amount of food in front of me. "I'll take a small scoop of eggs and a bagel, please. I'm not that hungry."

She hands me the plate, completely covered in scrambled eggs. "I'm Patty. Let me know if you need anything."

"Thank you," I smile, taking my tray of food with me. Stepping into the dining room, I'm surprised to see there are round tables throughout the room. This doesn't look anything like what I envisioned. Instead of long rectangular tables, connected end to end, the round tables are neatly covered in white tablecloths and set for six people. Anxiety instantly hits me. Do I sit by myself and seem anti-social, or do I sit with strangers and feel completely awkward?

"Celeste?" a familiar face calls from one of the tables on the other side of the room. Drake stands, waving me over to where he sits. I audibly sigh with the relief that floods me. Thank God, I don't have to choose. "Good morning," he says as I move closer. He stands as I approach, sliding a chair out for me to sit in.

"Good morning," I respond.

"You're an early riser, too?"

"I've never been good at sleeping," I lie, pretending to take a bite off the mound of eggs on my plate. "What about you?"

"Yeah, me neither. It used to drive my parents crazy. They tried everything to get me to sleep. Nothing worked. Finally, they gave up and let me stay up all night."

"All night? You don't sleep at all?"

"I sleep...I think." He shrugs. "Who knows?" He

takes a bite of bacon, crunching it loudly. "That was impressive yesterday."

I wrinkle my forehead, trying to figure out what he's talking about.

Drake scoffs. "The binary. You read it without inputting it into a computer."

"Oh, that." I wave my hand, dismissing his words. "It's nothing."

"Nothing? Let me repeat that. You read binary code without putting it into a computer." I pretend to eat my food, scooting it around on the plate. "I've never seen anyone do that before. It was impressive."

"Thank you." I don't know what to say. I watch him take another bite of bacon. His hair is the same color as my father's. So dark, it nearly looks black. High cheekbones are accentuated with a strong jaw and thick lips. He's handsome in a creature of the night kind of way. I smirk at my choice of words.

"Do I have food on my face?"

"What? No. Not that I see, why?"

"You were staring a hole through my face. I thought maybe part of my breakfast had taken up residence on my cheek."

"I'm sorry. I didn't mean to stare. You just remind me of someone."

He leans back, crossing his legs at the ankle. "I hope it's someone devilishly handsome." He laughs, patting his stomach. "Don't answer that." He stands, picking his tray up. "Are you ready or still eating?"

"I'm ready." I grab my tray and follow him to the window. I copy Drake's movements, dumping my eggs in the trash and sending my tray through the dishwasher.

"You'd think, as much as tuition costs for this place, they'd be able to afford someone to help Miss Patty in there." He points to the friendly lady at the counter. "She has to serve and clean up all by herself." He looks behind us. "Some of the brats that attend here think they shouldn't have to clean up after themselves and leave their trays where they sat."

"Really? That's rude. Why would they do that?"

"Because their shit doesn't stink."

I stare at Drake, trying to figure out what that means. This is precisely the reason I need to experience college. "Their shit doesn't smell?"

Drake laughs. "No, I'm sure it smells just like everyone else's. It's slang for someone thinking they're better than everyone else. Now that I think about it, that was pretty crude. Sorry."

I scoff. "Don't apologize. I've just never heard that saying before."

"Did someone keep you locked inside a tower?"

"Something like that." I laugh awkwardly.

"What time is your first class?"

I pull the printed schedule out of my backpack. "Eight o'clock. General English 201."

"I thought you were a freshman?"

"I am. Is that not a freshman course?"

"Not usually. 201 is a sophomore level. That's my first class, too."

"Do you mind if I walk with you?" I ask.

"Of course not, madam. I'd be proud to be your escort." He motions to the empty air in front of him. Drake's weird in a fun sort of way. I like it.

We walk into the main building, and with the club tables gone, I can see the beauty of the building. "This is magnificent." I recognize the architecture from the late nineteenth century.

"I know, right?" The wide staircase leads up from the landing. Both the stairs and the floor are made from Venetian marble. The walls are covered in a deep mahogany that glistens in the sunlight.

I glance at my watch, realizing we only have four minutes before class starts. "We need to hurry. We're going to be late."

"Mr. Morgan wouldn't know if we were late or not. He's kind of in his own world."

"Either way, I don't want to make a bad impression on the first day." We climb the ancient stairs, following a small crowd of students heading in the same direction.

"This is it." We stop in front of a wooden door that's at least nine feet tall, complete with a transom stained-glass window on top. As soon as we enter, I understand what Drake means. Nearly every desk in the room is full as the ancient professor stares out the large window that overlooks the parking circle. We find two seats next to each other in the back of the room and slide into them, trying not to draw attention to ourselves. I pull my laptop out of my backpack, and Drake's eyes open wide, giving me a silent warning.

"What is that?" the professor says from the front of the room. "Is that a computer in my classroom?" The man who was ignoring the class moments earlier is now honed in on my laptop.

"Yes, sir?"

Mr. Morgan slowly works his way to my seat, as every eye in the room follows his movement. As he approaches, their eyes switch from him to me.

"Put it away," Drake whispers.

I close the laptop quickly, sliding it back into my backpack, unsure of what's going on.

"Young lady," the professor announces, looming over my desk.

"Yes, sir?"

"Until computers are found to actually be beneficial in our world, they are outlawed in my classroom. Too many dangers from staring at the screens all day," he reprimands.

Is this man serious? Until computers are found to be beneficial? What century is he living in? I have a hard time holding in my laugh. I was born in the late 1300s, and I use computers. I can only imagine how he feels about microwaves.

"Yes, sir. I'm sorry. I didn't realize they weren't allowed. I won't bring it again."

"See that you don't, Miss…"

"Luquire," I fill in the blank.

"Miss Luquire. Welcome to Ravenwood." Mr. Morgan turns, heading back to the front of the room, taking the disapproving stares with him.

One glance at Drake and I can't control the smile. He's covering his face with a copy of *War and Peace*, and I swear tears are sliding down his cheeks. "Stop!" I whisper.

Thankfully, I survive an hour of the most boring lecture I've ever had the pleasure of listening to. Looking through the syllabus Mr. Morgan handed out midway through the lecture, I realize I've read every book listed, several times, making this even more boring than it should be.

When class is over, I follow Drake to the open hallway, pulling my schedule out. "It looks like biology is next, and I have two hours before it starts."

"Is there anything else I should know?"

"About your schedule?" he asks.

"I was thinking more along the lines of professors who believe computers are of the devil?"

Drake laughs. "No. Mr. Morgan is the only one. I should've warned you. Sorry about that. It was funny, though."

"I'm glad you were amused at my expense." I laugh with him.

"My next class is in ten minutes. I'll see you in algebra, Celeste." He turns, heading down the stairs.

With two hours to kill, I don't know what to do. I could go back to my room, but that's boring. Instead, I decide to head toward a few tables I noticed behind the dorms this morning. Moving through the crowd of students, I work my way behind the dorm. The moment I clear the crowd, I feel it.

A feeling I haven't felt since the night my father… since Viktor died. Someone is close. Someone I don't know, yet they share the same ability as me. I sniff the air, searching for the scent that piqued my attention initially. I smell it again. This time it's closer. "Where are you?" I whisper into the stillness. "I can feel you."

I turn, walking back toward the traffic circle, and the feeling lessens. Someone is in the woods. I quiet my movements, blending into the environment around me, and allow my senses to turn me into the predator I am.

A leaf cracks to my right. I turn, finding the space empty. A stick pops to my left. Again, I turn, finding nothing there. As quickly as the feeling appeared, it's gone. Whatever or whoever was here has gone. I sniff the air once more, finding the scent miles away.

It's possible they sensed me and left. There aren't a lot of us in this area, which is the main reason why I chose this school. As far as I know, I'm the only vampire at Ravenwood, for that matter, the only vampire in North Mississippi.

emeryn, the party animal

THERE ARE HALF AS many students in biology class as in English. Darby, the girl from the chess club table, motions me toward an empty desk next to hers. The professor is a middle-aged woman with once strawberry-blonde hair that's now turning white with age. She's on the plumper side, and her smile is warm and friendly. The class passes quickly and is much less painful to sit through than English.

"I'm starved," Darby announces. "Would you like to grab something to eat?"

I smile. "I'd love that, but I have one more class today."

"Seriously? How many hours are you taking?"

"Twenty-one."

Darby stares at me like I've lost my mind. "Were you trying to win some sort of championship in the first semester of your freshman year?"

"No?" I answer, not sure what she means.

"Twenty-one hours is suicidal. I don't take more than twelve a semester." She shrugs. "Also, that could explain why I'm taking a freshman-level biology course instead of the sophomore level I'm supposed to be in."

"Most of the classes I'm in won't take up much time."

Darby pulls my schedule from my hands. "You're a better person than me. These are all hard classes." We walk down the stairs to the second floor. "Algebra is on this floor. I'll see you later."

"Bye." I wave awkwardly.

Searching for the room number listed on my schedule, I find the door that matches almost at the end of the hall. "I think you're following me," a deep voice says from behind.

I turn, finding Drake. "You've got me. It was difficult to follow you by being in front, but I succeeded."

He reaches around me, opening the door wide. "Looks like you're stuck with me in this class, too." He smirks, raising one side of his mouth higher than the other.

"Is that a bad thing?" I ask.

"I hope not." He motions for me to enter. We find two seats in the middle of the class and sit quickly. The professor spends most of the time explaining his expectations and the syllabus to the class like he's speaking to kindergarten students instead of college freshmen. Toward the end of class, he asks everyone to complete a simple worksheet, testing our algebraic competency. I finish quickly and take it to his desk.

"Finished already?" he asks as I hand it to him.

"Yes, sir."

He slides his glasses down, covers his nose, and picks up my sheet. "Miss Luquire?" he turns toward me.

"Yes?"

"Excellent job. You may go."

I glance at Drake's paper on the way to my desk. He's almost finished and, from what I can tell, has all of them correct. He winks as I sling my backpack over my shoulder and leave algebra behind. I don't know whether to wait by the door or go downstairs. God, I hate social anxiety. You'd think someone who's been on Earth since medieval times would know how to talk to other people. Nope!

I decide to wait on the landing. It gives the look of "I wasn't waiting for you" while all the time I really was. Thankfully, Drake doesn't keep me waiting long. He's on the landing five minutes later.

"Numbers are your thing, aren't they?" he asks, moving toward me.

"Yeah, I guess. It was pretty easy. You finished quickly, too." He shrugs, leading me down the stairs.

"It's easy when you've taken the class before. It's taken me several times to be able to finish that quickly. You could say numbers are *not* my thing." I laugh, following him through the grand lobby and out the front doors. "Are you hungry?"

"Yes," I lie.

"Would you like to get something with me?"

"Sure. Where should we go?"

Drake laughs. "I was thinking the dining hall would be a good choice. I hear they serve an amazing hamburger steak."

"Sold." I laugh, walking beside him to the building across from the dorms.

He opens the door for me to enter when the feeling from yesterday hits me again. This time it's stronger. I stop, looking around for anything out of the ordinary.

"Celeste? Are you okay?" I ignore Drake's words, focusing on the energy. It's coming from the same area as yesterday. I turn, heading behind the dorm. "Celeste?" Drake calls, staying right on my heels. "What's going on? We don't have to eat in the dining hall. Although I don't have anything to eat in my dorm room."

As quickly as it came, it disappears. Living in a city saturated with vampires, I'm used to feeling strange and unusual energies. I don't recognize this person's energy, and that makes me uneasy.

"Celeste?" Drake touches my shoulder, and the pulse that flowed between us the first time we touched intensifies, as it flows from my shoulder to my toes. I step away, almost tripping over my feet.

"You shocked me again."

Drake pulls his hand away, staring at it blankly. "Why is that happening?"

"You tell me. It came from you."

He steps away. "Did it hurt?"

"It didn't feel great," I admit.

"I'm so sorry." He steps closer, stopping before he touches me. "I understand if you want to take a rain check on dinner."

"No, it's fine."

"Why are we staring into the empty woods?" he asks.

I turn back toward the shadowed trees. "I thought I heard something." I face him. "Never mind. It must have been my imagination. Ready to eat?"

He follows me into the cafeteria without another word.

Patty greets us as we approach. Apparently, we're late for dinner, and there's not much to choose from. When it's my turn, I choose the smallest piece of hamburger steak in the pan and a tiny spoonful of mashed potatoes. "Are you sure you don't want anything else?" Miss Patty asks.

"No, I'm good. This will be more than enough." I follow Drake to the table that's furthest away from the few remaining students.

"You didn't get much food," Drake notices.

"I'm not that hungry." I shove the food around on my plate. "We need to talk about why you keep shocking me. You felt it too. I could tell."

He sets his fork on the edge of his plate. "I don't know what you're talking about."

Making sure no one is around, I scoot forward in my chair. Trying a technique that I witnessed my father do on many occasions, I stare into his eyes. Focusing his attention solely on me. "Where are you from, Drake?"

"Alabama," he answers.

"More specific," I demand.

"Mobile, Alabama."

I move even closer, holding his gaze in mine. "What are you?"

He takes a deep breath and shrugs. "Human?"

"What?"

He takes a bite from his tray. "You asked what I was. I answered."

Why am I confused? "You didn't feel anything when we were walking outside?"

"Are you coming on to me, Celeste? I mean, I'm not against it, but it's a little sudden, don't you think?"

I stand, grab my tray, and head toward the dishwasher. I've never technically done the hypnotizing thing before, but I'm a damn ancient vampire. The oldest in Louisiana. There's no way that wouldn't have worked. Is he immune? Is that a thing?

"Celeste?" Drake runs up behind me. "Did I say something wrong?"

"No. I'm tired and need to study. I'll see you tomorrow." I leave him standing in place.

I stomp my way across the drive and into the dorm room to find my temperamental roommate sitting at her desk. "Hi-de-ho, roomie," Emeryn greets me. "How was the first day?"

I drop my backpack and collapse on my bed. "It sucked. How was yours?"

She shrugs. "I don't know. I choose not to participate in the first-day rituals. I'll go tomorrow."

"Doesn't that make tomorrow your first day, which theoretically cancels out your nonparticipation?"

"Damn. You're right. Looks like tomorrow is out too."

I watch as she attempts to follow a YouTube video on makeup application. She's wiped her eye clean at least five times and keeps rewinding the video. "What are you working on?" I ask from my side of the room.

"The notorious smoky eye. I've tried to master it for the past year. I get super close but then end up looking like a clown."

"I've never been good at makeup."

Emeryn stops the video and turns toward me. "You're kidding, right? Your makeup is flawless. And whatever you do for your skincare routine, you need to share."

I face the girl who wanted nothing to do with me earlier. "You mean that?"

She shrugs. "I wouldn't have said it if I didn't." She pushes play and continues blending different shades of black and gray together on her eyelids.

"I just have good genes."

"Yeah, well, you've got me beat there. I have the genes of a demon and a troll."

I sit up. "Seriously?"

Emeryn huffs a laugh. "Not technically, but it feels that way." She turns, continuing her makeup. "You didn't think my parents were actually a demon and a troll, did you?"

"No," I lie. I've been here for two days, and I'm already discovering just how naive I am. I've lived in a vampire bubble of protection my entire life. My phone buzzes, and my eyes fill with tears, seeing the message from Fran. I never imagined I'd miss her as much as I do.

How are you?

I'm good

I lie again. That's twice in the last minute.

My classes are great, and I've already made a friend.

That's great, sweetheart. I knew you'd fit in quickly.

I miss you.

I miss you, too. I'll see you soon. I promise.

Fran doesn't send any more texts, and I'm regretting this decision to attend college. What was I thinking?

"Want to go into town?" Emeryn interrupts my internal pity party.

"What?"

"Town. With me. Want to go?" she repeats.

"We can do that?"

She laughs, finishing her second smoky eye. "This is college, not a prison. We can leave anytime we want."

"How are we going to get there?"

She pulls a set of keys from her desk and flashes an evil smile. "I have a car."

"What do you have in mind?" I ask.

"There's a bar not too far from here. I saw it when we came to visit the campus." She stands. "Put on something slutty, and let's go." Ten minutes later, I'm wearing the sluttiest outfit I have and ready to go. "That's it, huh?" Emeryn asks, assessing my clothing choices.

I look down at the black leather pants and red tank top I'm wearing. "Is this not slutty enough?"

"No, the outfit is good, but you need to change the shoes. UGG boots don't work with leather pants."

I switch them out for a pair of red heels that I originally ignored because they feel like a pair of torture devices attached to my feet.

"Yep. That's it. Sluttiness level achieved. Pull your hair out of that ponytail, and you'll be ready." I do as she suggests, letting my red curls hang halfway down my back.

"Why do I feel like I'm doing something bad?" I whisper as we head down the stairs and out into the night.

"Because you're a good girl who's never broken the rules." I follow her to the parking lot, which feels at least a mile away from the dorm. She's right. I've spent my entire life following every rule my father set for me and doing exactly what was expected of me. Now that I'm not trapped in the body of a five-year-old, it's time to live my life.

We reach the car, just as my feet feel like they're about to fall off my body. Emeryn clicks a button, and a car roars to life. "This is your car?" I ask, staring at the green sports car in front of me.

"Yep. My mother enjoys spending my inheritance."

a dive bar in rural mississippi

ONE OF THE main reasons I chose Ravenwood was the privacy and reputation. It's a university, but its remote location and small size was just what I was looking for. I expected to spend my days in the library, pretending to study, and my nights hanging out with the other girls, giggling about boys and other silly issues. Riding in a high-dollar sports car, being driven by an angsty teenager, wasn't even on the radar.

I grab the bar above the window as Emeryn pushes the car faster than she should. "Why are you hanging on so tightly?" she asks, turning the radio to full blast.

I laugh awkwardly. "I'm not trying to die today."

She lets the driver's side window down and lets out a high-pitched squeal. "This is what I needed!"

Ten minutes later, the car pulls to a stop in front of a building that resembles a shack rather than a bar. "Is this the bar?"

"Yep. At least I think so." The moment we step out of the car, I feel an energy I haven't felt for a while. There are lycan here. "You good?" Emeryn asks, noticing I'm not moving.

"I'm good," I lie. Please don't let this wolf be someone who knows me. The parking lot is full of motorcycles and older model trucks. I have a feeling we're about to walk into somewhere we're not going to be welcomed. "Emeryn? Have you been here before?"

"Nope. There's a first time for everything."

"Maybe we should go somewhere a little more... modern?"

"This place is perfect." She wraps her arm through mine, pulling me toward the rickety front porch. "Maybe they'll have karaoke."

I sigh, letting her pull me up the stairs toward the entrance. The moment we walk inside, the room goes silent, and every eye turns toward us. Every person staring could be the energy I'm sensing.

"Hi!" Emeryn waves at the patrons. "What's a girl gotta do to get a drink around here?" Oh, my God. I want to hide from secondhand embarrassment.

"A girl's gotta be over twenty-one," a voice says from across the room.

Emeryn pulls an ID out of her designer handbag, holding it in the air. "Will twenty-two work?"

"Bring it over here," an older woman says from behind the bar. I follow Emeryn to the woman and watch as she flips the ID on top of the bar proudly. The woman studies it, looking for any clues to her true age. "It looks legit." She turns to me. "What about you?"

"Oh, I'm not going to be drinking."

"She's twenty-one. She forgot her ID tonight. We realized after it was too late to turn back."

"She can sit with you, but I'm not serving her." The older woman wipes the counter clean in front of two empty barstools. "Sit," she demands.

"That's fine," I answer. "I'm not thirsty." Behind us, conversations continue throughout the room. I tune into each, listening for anything that might cause us issues. Most of the people are talking about us, but nothing out of the ordinary.

"What do you want to drink?" the bartender asks Emeryn.

"A cosmopolitan, please." Emeryn slaps a twenty-dollar bill on the bar top.

"Look around, sweet cheeks. Does it look like we serve cosmopolitans in here?"

Emeryn smiles. "Beer, please."

"What kind?"

"You choose," she answers. The older woman sets a bottle of beer in front of Emeryn and takes the money before walking away.

"Isn't this great?" she whispers.

"No. These people are not happy we're here."

It doesn't take long before two younger men sit on either side of us. The lycan energy they bring with them is nearly overwhelming. "What are a couple of ladies like you doing in a dive like this?" the guy next to me asks. His southern accent is thicker than I've heard in a while.

"We're looking for a little fun," Emeryn answers, stretching over me.

"I'm Jackson. That's Jasper."

"Double J's. I like it. You aren't twins, are you?" Emeryn laughs, and I cringe internally.

"Only if you two are," Jackson answers. Music blares over a jukebox in the back corner, and Emeryn sets her beer down.

"Let's dance!" She stands, trying to pull me with her.

"No. I'm not into dancing. You go."

"I'll dance with you." Jackson stands, taking her hand into his. I watch them go to the center of the room and attempt some sort of line dance with two other dancers.

"I'm sorry about him. He can be a little over the top," Jasper says, sliding to the stool next to me.

"It's fine. Emeryn is grown. She can handle herself."

"That's more than I can say about Jackson. He's a six-year-old trapped in a twenty-two-year-old body. I have to watch him constantly. I'm basically his babysitter."

I turn, facing Jasper. Is he the lycanthrope? I look into his bright blue eyes, searching for clues and not finding any. "Emeryn is my roommate. It appears I'm going to have to babysit her, as well."

"Maybe we can start a club." He laughs.

"I believe that's been done."

"Can I buy you a drink?" Jasper asks.

"No, I don't drink. I'm here to make sure Emeryn doesn't end up a statistic."

He turns toward the two of them on the dance floor. "Jackson will pass out before too much longer, and she won't have to worry about him."

"Is he a threat?"

Jasper scoffs. "A threat? He'd like to think he is, but no. He's harmless." Several minutes of awkward silence pass between us. "Are you two in college?"

"Yeah. We attend Ravenwood."

"Oh, I've seen that place. It's always kind of reminded me of a boarding school for rich brats." He turns toward me. "I don't mean you're a rich brat."

"No offense taken. I'm sure there are a few of those on campus. I've only been there a few days. What about you? Do you go to college?"

He laughs. "No. College isn't on my career path. I work for my father."

"What's he do?"

"He's the supervisor for a local company."

I nod. "That sounds interesting."

"Not really. It's a family business, and I don't have much of a choice in my future employment."

"I can understand that. Sometimes, making our own choices can be hard."

"What about you? Where are you from?"

"New Orleans."

"The Big Easy," he answers. "I love that city. We go down there at least twice a year. My dad has meetings we're required to attend."

Emeryn and Jackson come back to the bar, both breathing hard and laughing. "Come on. You two need to dance with us."

"I'm game if you are," Jasper says.

"Okay." I came to college for the experience. This is as good a place to start as any. I follow Jasper to the dance floor, and we join the small group in the middle. A familiar song comes on, and I attempt to follow the steps that Emeryn magically knows.

It doesn't take long to feel the groove of the music. I'm actually enjoying line dancing in a dump of a bar in rural Mississippi. The song ends, and Jackson wraps his arms around Emeryn. Thankfully, Jasper doesn't imitate his movements as the four of us move back toward the bar, where Emeryn finishes her beer.

"How about we get out of here?" Jackson asks. "I know a place where we can have some privacy."

"That sounds like a good idea," Emeryn answers.

"We're good here," I interrupt. "Emeryn, we should think about getting back before too much longer."

"The night's still young," she sways from her stool, nearly falling off. "Whoops." She giggles. "I think I'm drunk."

"You've had one beer. You're not drunk."

Jasper sniffs the empty beer bottle. "There's more in

this bottle than beer." He turns toward the bartender. "Who came over here while we were dancing?"

"I have better things to do than to babysit people's drinks." She moves over to a group of older men at the end of the bar. They're staring at the four of us.

"What's wrong?" I ask.

"Someone drugged your friend," Jasper answers. "We need to get her out of here."

"We just got here," Emeryn complains. "I'm having fun."

"Well, you won't be having fun for much longer. Do you have the keys?" Grabbing her purse off her shoulder, I pull out the familiar key fob and shake it at him. "Is that a Porsche emblem?"

"Shit. Who would've done this?" Jackson asks.

"Assholes," Jasper answers. "We need to get her out of here." He turns toward me. "Can you drive?"

I shake my head. "No. I never learned."

"She's in no condition to drive anywhere." Jasper sighs. "Okay. I can drive you back. Jackson can follow us on his bike and bring me back here to get mine."

"Are you sure you want to do that?"

He turns toward Emeryn, who is now passed out and being held up by Jackson. "I don't think we have much of a choice."

"Okay."

Jackson carries Emeryn outside, stopping when he sees the car lights flash. "That's your car?"

"No, it's Emeryn's."

"Damn." He carries her to the car, gently laying her in the backseat. "Makes my Kia look rough." I climb into the passenger seat, and Jasper slides into the driver's seat.

"I've never driven anything like this." He looks over at me. "In case you're wondering, I'm not going to hurt you."

"I know," I answer. He couldn't hurt me if he wanted to. It's Emeryn I'm worried about. He pushes the button, and the car roars to life. Jasper pulls the Porsche onto the road, and a single headlight follows behind us.

"I'll admit. This isn't where I thought the night would be taking me."

"You and me, both." I laugh. "I've never been to a place like that. It was fun while it lasted."

Jasper laughs. "I find it hard to believe you've never been to a bar before. You live in the City of Sin."

"I had an overprotective parent," I answer.

"I know how that goes." Jasper is driving much more calmly than Emeryn did earlier. The lycanthrope energy is still near, and for some reason, I'm having trouble distinguishing if it's Jackson or Jasper. I haven't spent much time with wolves, maybe that's why their energy is hard to pinpoint.

"I don't think it's a good idea for the two of you to go into that bar again."

"I agree. Whether Emeryn will agree is a different story."

He turns, looking at my passed-out roommate. "You're going to have to convince her." He pulls the sports car into the parking lot we left less than an hour ago, and the motorcycle pulls in after. "Do you need help getting her to your room?"

"I think I can do it. Thank you." I reach over, touching his shoulder, and the energy that rushes through me is instant. Jasper feels it too. He takes a deep breath, and his blue eyes begin to glow.

"What are you?" he asks.

I smile. "I think you know."

He sniffs the air, raising his nose high. "I knew you smelled different, but I never would've thought you were a...a vampire."

"It took me until now to realize you were the lycanthrope I was sensing."

"What do we do now?" Jasper asks, staring at me.

"Are you asking me if we're supposed to fight until the death?"

He smiles. "I don't know what I'm asking."

I step out of the car, and Jasper does the same. "It was a pleasure to meet you, Jasper, the lycanthrope."

"I don't know your name," he admits.

"Celeste."

"It was nice to meet you, Celeste, the vampire." He heads toward the motorcycle and climbs behind Jackson. I watch as the two of them leave the parking lot, heading in the direction of the bar.

Thankful for my nonhuman strength, I lift Emeryn

from the backseat and throw her over my shoulder. The heels she made me wear make the journey harder than it should be. I move at vampire speed toward the dorm, only slowing down when I enter the campus grounds. I don't bother to undress her before putting her in bed and collapsing on mine.

dr. oliver fitzgerald

I GET ready for class before Emeryn is awake. Not only is she still wearing the same clothes she partied in, but she hasn't switched positions all night. I resist the urge to check on her and make sure she's not in some drug-induced coma. Truthfully, I'm annoyed at her. Even I would've known better than to drink a drink I left alone in a strange bar. Last night could've turned out much worse than it did.

Instead of going to the cafeteria, I head to the picnic tables I saw the other day and never made it to. Autumn in Mississippi is similar to autumn in New Orleans. Nonexistent. It's hot and sticky, making it feel like June instead of late September. I pick a spot in the shade and pull out a novel from my backpack. The campus is quiet since most people are still asleep. I don't get very far in the chapter when the energy from yesterday rushes me again. This time it's not far away. I jump to my feet, turning in every direction, and search for the source.

In an instant, a man I recognize from New Orleans is standing in front of me. He's tall, well-dressed, and a vampire.

"What do you want?" I hiss.

He holds his hands in front of his chest. "I'm not here to harm you, Celeste Luquire." Every part of me is at attention, ready for whatever is about to happen.

"How did you find me?"

"I'm here for a reason other than the immortal child of Viktor Luquire. I was as surprised as you to find you were attending the university."

"May I sit?" I shrug. Oliver sits, crossing his legs. "I was there that night."

"What night?"

"The night your father died, and the night you..."

I slide my book into my backpack and throw it over my shoulder. "It was nice speaking with you, Mr. Fitzgerald. This conversation is over. Perhaps we'll see each other again."

"Good day, Miss Luquire." I leave the vampire at the table and head straight to the cafeteria. I bypass the food line, heading to a table in the back corner. He knows my truth. The last time he saw me I was in the body of a five-year-old.

"Are you okay?" a voice interrupts my thoughts. I look up to find Drake standing a few feet in front of me.

"I'm fine."

He's holding a food tray. "Mind if I sit here?"

"No, go for it."

"Want to talk about it?" he asks.

"About what?"

Drake scoffs. "Whatever is making your face look like your best friend just died."

I slide back in my seat. "No."

"Do you want me to leave?"

I sigh. "No, please stay. I'm afraid I'm not going to be good at conversation this morning."

"Then I'll eat while you think." His energy is calming, and I'm grateful he found me. He finishes eating quickly and dumps his tray.

"Want to walk to English together?"

"I'd like that. Thank you." I grab my backpack and follow him out of the room. I feel Oliver's energy, still. He's somewhere on campus, making the anxiety return.

"I don't know what's going on, Celeste. But if you need to talk about it, I'm here." He hands me a piece of paper with a number written on it. "Here's my cell. Text me anytime."

"Thank you." We enter the building and climb the three flights of stairs. Oliver's energy grows the further we climb. We enter the room, finding the same two desks we sat in the first day of class.

Ten minutes later, Mr. Morgan still hasn't shown up, and whispers pass around the classroom on whether we can leave or not. Just as several students get up, the door opens, and Oliver walks in. Shit.

"Good morning, students. I'm afraid Mr. Morgan has fallen ill. I will be filling in for the rest of the semester." Several girls in the class sit straighter, combing through their already perfect hair with their fingers. "My name is Dr. Fitzgerald, and I've had the pleasure of teaching English at several colleges and universities around the South."

"I wonder if old Mr. Morgan kicked the bucket?" Drake interrupts my panic attack. I don't answer.

The hour passes quickly, and Oliver, surprisingly, is good at teaching English. I jump to my feet the second class is over.

"Miss Luquire. Please stay after class."

Drake looks at me, wrinkling his forehead. "Do you know him?"

"No."

"Want me to wait with you?" he asks.

"No, I'll be fine. I'll see you at Algebra."

Drake doesn't look convinced but doesn't push the issue. "Text me if you need anything." He makes eye contact with Oliver, sending an unwarranted threat.

Once the room is empty and the door is closed, I make my way to the front of the room. "What do you want?"

He sighs, sitting at his desk. "After our brief interaction this morning, I wanted to clear the air between us. I'm filling in at Ravenwood for a matter that has nothing to do with you. As far as I'm concerned, you're just another student in my English class. I will admit, my curiosity is aroused about all of this," he circles his finger from my head to toe, "but that isn't my concern right now. I trusted your father, as I will trust you." He slides a few papers into his shoulder bag. "I hope one day you will feel safe enough to tell me how this came about. Until then, your secret is safe with me."

I stare at the vampire in front of me. "Thank you," I whisper.

"Have a good day, Miss Luquire. Don't forget to do your homework."

"I could teach the class." I turn, walking away with two hours to kill before Biology. I exit the ancient house and return to the dorm, feeling the need to check on Emeryn.

Entering the room, I'm surprised to find her sitting on the edge of her bed. "Are you okay?"

"What happened?"

I throw my backpack on the floor next to my bed and flop on top. "Someone drugged you."

She stands, wobbling slightly. "I was roofied?" I shrug, not knowing what that means. "How did I get here?"

"Jasper and Jackson."

"Oh, God. This is getting worse by the minute. My car?"

"In the parking lot, safe."

Emeryn rubs her head dramatically. "I feel like an elephant is sitting on top of me."

"Did Jackson drug me?"

"No. It happened while you were dancing with him. He wouldn't have had the chance."

"Good, I liked him."

I stand, moving to her side. "Don't get any ideas of going back there. That place is dangerous. Who knows what would've happened to you if it weren't for the two of them."

"I need a shower." She grabs her shower bucket and heads down the hallway.

Being the rule follower I am, I grab my bag and head toward biology class. Darby is already in the room, holding the empty desk for me. "Good morning, sunshine." She smiles as she greets me.

"It's something," I answer. Biology is easy, and the professor has moved to the top of my favorite professor list. Her energy is warm and loving. In fact, I'm not happy when it's time to leave.

"Have fun in Algebra," Darby says as she heads to the first floor. I head toward the room, finding Drake leaning against the wall outside the door.

"Were you waiting on me?" I ask.

"Maybe." He smiles. "Everything okay with Dr. Fitzgerald?"

I return his smile. "Yes. Nothing major. He wanted to ask me about a note Mr. Morgan left in the lesson plans."

"Don't tell me that old coot kept a record of you bringing your laptop out in his class."

"Something like that." I smile. "Ready for Algebra?"

"No." He follows me inside the room.

The professor spends a short amount of time lecturing on the importance of algebra in the workplace today, before solving a problem on the board and asking us to repeat the process with similar problems. Glancing around the classroom, most of the students look confused at his halfhearted instructions. I resist the urge to reteach the skill and complete the assignment quickly. The professor smiles, taking the sheet from me. On the way to the door, I hand Drake a piece of paper with my number scribbled on it and leave him alone to fight the numbers.

The moment I exit the building, I feel lycan energy. It feels like the same energy as last night. I follow the energy, working my way through campus and into the parking lot. Leaning against an older model truck, I find the source, Jasper. His arms and ankles are crossed, and he's wearing a smirk across his face.

"What are you doing here, wolf?"

"I couldn't sleep last night, thinking about a vampire that didn't know how to drive." He stands straight, towering over me. "I thought I'd fix that today. I need my beauty sleep."

"You're going to teach me how to drive?" I scoff.

"I'm going to try." He slides into the passenger seat, closing the door behind him. "Get in!" he mouths through the closed window.

He can't be serious. I'm going to learn to drive on an

ancient truck? I don't move. Jasper opens the door. "You getting in or what?"

"You're serious?"

"Do I look serious?"

I move to the driver's door and throw my backpack inside. Climbing behind the steering wheel, I start the truck like I've seen Fran do a million times. "You've got that part mastered. Now, put your foot on the brake, and shift into drive."

I look around the dash, locating the gear shifter. I follow orders and slowly shift the truck into drive.

"Put your foot on the gas, and get us out of the parking lot." I push the pedal, and the truck lunges forward. "A little softer than that. You want to push it down, but not that hard."

I try again. This time the truck slowly starts moving. "Good. Now, pull out onto the road and drive."

"Are you sure?"

"Is that a vampire thing? Asking the same question, over and over?"

"I could tear your arms off before you realized I moved," I warn.

"If you did that, who would teach you how to drive?"

I laugh. "Good point."

"The brake pedal is on the left, and the gas is on the right. Relax. Driving is easy." I take a deep breath and pull onto the road. My hands are tense, and the muscles in my arms are tight as I grip the steering wheel with enough force to rip it from the dash.

"Good," he says. "Now, can we go a little faster than twenty?" I push the truck up to fifty miles an hour and begin feeling more confident by the second.

"This is pretty easy," I confess.

"Yep. You're a quick learner." He points to a sign on the side of the road. "Turn by that sign. There's a lake back there that's beautiful."

"You're not going to take me back there and try to take advantage of me, are you?"

Jasper laughs. "You just threatened to rip my arms off. I'm not an idiot. You're stronger than me, and I'm okay with that."

I slow down, but not quite enough. As I turn, the back end of the truck slides to the side, before righting itself. "Oh, my God. What did I do?"

"You took the corner a little too fast and drifted the rear end. It's good. We're okay. Next time you turn a corner, you might want to slow down a little more. Keep following this road. It'll dead end into the water."

The dirt road stops, changing into nothing but grass as the lake comes into view. Giant pine trees surround the lake, making it hidden from view. "Stop right there." He points at a bare spot near the water.

"Are you sure *I* should drive that close?"

"You've got this." I slow down, pulling the truck into the exact location he wants. "You did it. Make sure you put it in park."

He hops out and pulls the tailgate down before I get my door open. I move to the back of the truck to find him sitting on the tailgate, staring at the water. "This is my favorite spot in the world." He pats to the open space beside him. I hop up, staring into the clear water.

"This is beautiful," I agree. I take a deep breath, inhaling the smell of pine. "Do you come here a lot?"

He lays back, staring at the clouds above. "I did when I was younger. Lately, I haven't had much time." He turns toward me. "What's your story, Celeste?"

"I don't have a story."

He laughs. "I don't believe that for one minute. Everyone has a story. I have a feeling yours is more interesting than most."

"Why, because I'm a vampire?"

He shrugs. "Yes, and no."

I lay back in the truck, mimicking his moves. "Well. My parents are dead, and I'm on my own."

"By parents, do you mean the vampire that made you a vampire?"

I don't know this man well enough to tell him about my life. I choose the expected answer and lie. "Yes. They were the ones who made me."

"How old are you?"

"Eighteen," I lie again.

"How long have you been on earth?"

"Nearly eight hundred years."

Jasper sits up. "That's nearly a millennium."

I nod.

"Why the hell are you in college?"

"The experience."

"Aren't you afraid you might slip up and eat someone?"

I laugh. "I don't drink human blood."

"Is that possible?"

"I've drank goat blood since being turned." *Mostly...*

Jasper lays back in the truck bed. "You know how many stereotypes you're ruining for me?"

"I hope all of them." I pause. "What about you? I'm guessing that family business has something to do with the lycan."

"My father is the Alpha of North Mississippi. There aren't a ton of lycan in the area, but it keeps him busy."

"Does that mean you'll be Alpha one day?"

He scoffs. "No, that honor is bestowed on my older brother. I believe you met him last night."

I turn, facing him. "Jackson? He is the future Alpha?" I can't stop the laugh that forms.

"Go ahead, get it out. I'd laugh too if I were you." He sighs, resting his head on his hands.

"I didn't pick up on him being a lycanthrope, but I did you."

"What does that mean?" Jasper asks.

I shrug. "Who knows?" My phone buzzes.

Are you okay? This is Drake, BTW

I'm good. Thanks for checking on me.

"Boyfriend?"

"No, just a friend. I should get back. I need to make sure Emeryn's still alive." I jump out of the back of the truck. "The sun is going down. Maybe you should drive us back."

"Nope. It's all you." He closes the tailgate and hurries to the passenger seat.

The drive back to the university is quiet, and the energy between us is easy. My dad was friends with Edon, the Alpha of New Orleans. Whenever they met at our home, he sent me upstairs to hide. Being around a lycanthrope is a new experience for me. Except for the one I killed. I push that memory from my mind.

"You're quiet over there. Is everything okay?"

I smile. "I'm good. Just thinking."

"Of ways to kill me?"

"We already discussed this. You'd be dead before you knew I was coming."

Jasper laughs. "Oh, that's right. I keep forgetting."

I turn into the small parking area, pulling into an empty spot next to Emeryn's Porsche. "Thank you for teaching me to drive, Jasper."

"It was my pleasure. You're far from an expert, so don't go taking off in that Porsche anytime soon." He jumps out of the truck and opens my door before I realize what he's doing. "Can I walk you to your dorm?"

"Thank you for the offer, but I'll be fine." He closes the door behind me. "Thank you for today, Jasper the wolf."

"Thank you, Celeste, the vampire."

It's not until I'm near the dorms that I hear the engine of the truck start. I round the corner to find Drake, sitting on the front steps.

things that howl in the night

"CELESTE. IS EVERYTHING OKAY?" Drake stands the moment he sees me, moving toward me.

"I'm good. I just needed some air."

He looks down, kicking at a piece of grass. "Do you want to grab something to eat?"

"No, I'm not hungry, but thank you for the invitation. I need to check on Emeryn. She wasn't feeling well earlier."

"Okay. Let me know if you need anything."

I turn, heading upstairs and to the room at the end of the hall. Unlocking the door, I find Emeryn back in bed. "Emeryn?" I move to her side, nudging her shoulder. "Emeryn?"

She moans. "What?"

"Are you okay?"

"Yeah. I took a shower and then a nap."

"Emeryn, it's eight o'clock at night. You slept the entire day."

She sits up. Her hair is sticking out in all directions, and her smokey eye has turned into a smokey face. "Are you fucking kidding me?" Her words are slurred.

"Let me get you something to drink." I grab water from her mini fridge and force her to drink it.

"Why didn't you wake me?"

"I did...this morning."

"Do you remember me telling you someone drugged you?"

She scratches her head. "I think so. Is that what's wrong with me?"

"I guess so. Maybe you should go see the nurse."

"No. I feel better after drinking that. I need some food."

I scrounge through her food bucket and find a candy bar. "Eat this. The sugar will help." She takes the bar, eating it in one bite.

"I think I need another shower." She stands, heading toward the bathroom. If I were human, I would be worried about the length of time she's been passed out. Tuning in to her blood flow, I can hear that she's fine and seems to be improving. When she finally returns, she seems more like herself.

"Feeling better?"

"Yes. I don't know what kind of drug that was, but damn, lesson learned." She sets her shower bucket down. "How did you get me into bed?"

I shrug. "I carried you."

Emeryn scoffs. "You must be stronger than you look. I've decided I'm swearing off bars for a while."

"That's definitely for the best. Do you remember anything from last night?"

She sits on the edge of her bed. "After we danced and I finished off my beer, no. Thanks for taking care of me."

"You're welcome."

"God, why am I still so sleepy?" She collapses on her bed.

"Get some rest. I'm not going anywhere."

"Thanks, Celeste. I have to go to class tomorrow." She sighs, sliding back underneath her covers.

My phone buzzes.

How's Emeryn?

> She's tired but better. Thanks for checking.

See you for breakfast tomorrow?

> Sure. See you then.

I set my phone down and curl underneath the covers of the bed I don't sleep in. Emeryn's breathing has slowed down, and she's snoring lightly. I pull out my laptop and begin searching for information on the Alpha of North Mississippi. It only takes a few searches and a short dive through the dark web to find information on the bar that I'm sure serves as their headquarters. A picture of a man in his late forties pulls up on my screen, and immediately, I know he's Jasper's father. They share the same bright blue eyes and dark hair. I wonder if he knew Edon?

I search a bit more, finding information on his family. Eventually, I come across a family photo of the entire family. Jackson and Jasper are standing side by side, both look to be barely teenagers. If they're in birth order, Jasper is next in line for Alpha behind Jackson. The old picture is the only thing I'm able to find, and I stop searching, not sure what else there is to know.

I change tactics, searching instead for Oliver Fitzgerald. Like a typical vampire, there's not much information to be found. The only thing available is a picture from Loyola University, which is a listing of their part-time professors. Oliver is standing in front of the familiar building with a smile on his face. "Why are you here, Oliver?" I whisper to no one.

God, I miss my father. He would have all the answers. I think back to life in New Orleans and decide to call someone I haven't talked to since *that* night. The night that Viktor, my father, died. The night I ended as a five-year-old immortal child. Stepping out of the room, I make my way downstairs to the front of the dorm. Thankfully, the moon is full, and the campus is quiet.

The phone barely rings once before she answers. *"Celeste?"*

"It's me," I answer.

"Oh, my God. Are you alright? I haven't heard anything from you since..." she doesn't complete the sentence. *"I've been worried sick."*

"I know. I'm sorry. I should've kept in contact. I just..."

"I know," she interrupts.

"You sound so..."

"Grown-up?" I smile at my words.

"Yes. How?"

"Pretty much the same way as the last time. However, it's a different spell, and the conditions are different."

"What are the conditions?" she asks.

I don't answer. Now is not the time to think about all that. Instead, I change the subject. *"I have a question about Oliver Fitzgerald."*

"Ollie? What about him?" I sigh, not sure how much I want to disclose about my location. *"Celeste. You know you can trust me, right? You're my maker, and we're joined eternally. I love you."*

"I'm at college in Mississippi. Oliver showed up yesterday as an English professor."

Amelia laughs loudly. *"Oh, my God. He did that to me, too, when I went undercover to catch the cult."*

"Is he here to find me?"

"I doubt it has anything to do with you. If you're anywhere near Natchez, that's his hometown. Want me to ask him what he's up to?"

"No! I don't want him to know we talked."

She laughs. "I'm good at using words. He'll never know a thing."

"Okay. One more thing."

"Anything," she answers.

"Are you still with that wolf guy?"

"Topher?" she giggles. "Yes. Since Edon died, he became the Alpha of New Orleans. We're married now."

"Oh, my God. You're married? I should've been there. I'm so sorry."

She's quiet for a minute. "Don't apologize. I understand."

"Do you think he knows anything about the Alpha of North Mississippi?"

"I'll ask when he gets home. Have you met some of the lycan from that area?"

I sigh. "Two brothers. I'm trying to find information on them."

"I'll find out and let you know. If there's anything you need to know, you'll be the first one I call."

"Thank you, Amelia. I'm sorry I haven't contacted you sooner."

"I miss you." Her voice is soft.

"I miss you, too. Let me know what he says. You can call me at this number anytime."

"I will. Bye, Celeste. I love you." The phone goes silent before I can respond. Hearing her voice brings back memories of my father's death. I wipe a silent tear and place that memory in the back of my mind. Now is not the time to travel that path.

A faint howl echoes through my ears. So soft, human ears would never notice. I freeze in place, waiting for the sound to repeat. Several minutes later, I'm rewarded with another faint howl.

Without thinking, I take off, moving toward the source, and within minutes, I'm behind the dive bar from last night. I stop, listening again. This time it's louder, still in the distance. I keep running, moving toward the source. The next time I stop, I realize I'm near the lake where Jasper brought me earlier.

The howl sounds again, this time much closer. I move to the opposite edge of the water, arriving just as the howl sounds again. Sensing they're closer, I jump high into a tree. Underneath, the sound of cracking leaves causes the hairs on my arms to stand at attention.

Out of the corner of my eye, I see it. A large black wolf stalks closer to the tree. It continues until it's directly beneath my hiding spot. Its nose lifts high in the air, and it sniffs in my direction. I shrink further into the foliage, blending in with my environment. It shifts slightly, staring into my hiding spot. Bright blue eyes sparkle in the moonlight, and he licks his lips.

Out of nowhere, a second wolf, larger than the first, jumps on the first, and the two begin to wrestle. They stop moments later and howl loudly at the full moon hanging over the lake.

I know without asking that I've just seen Jackson and Jasper in wolf form. There's something about the freedom they're experiencing that brings a smile to my face. I watch the two of them run away and wait until the howls are far in the distance before leaving my hiding place.

I arrive back at the dorm in less than a second. The campus looks the same as it did earlier. There are no sounds, no movement, no nothing.

Back in the room, Emeryn is miraculously somehow still asleep, and I've researched everything I can think to research on lycan, the Alpha of North Mississippi, and Oliver Fitzgerald.

Thankfully, the sun begins to peek over the horizon, which means life has resumed around me. Emeryn yawns and stretches, pulling her hands high over her head. "How do you feel?" I ask.

"Good. I feel human again. Whatever some asshat drugged me with has finally worn off."

"Going to class today?"

She sighs. "Sadly." She pulls her phone in front of her face dramatically. "That guy from the bar texted me."

"Jackson?"

She drops her phone on the bed. "I don't even remember giving him my number."

I try not to act too interested. "What did he want?"

She pulls the phone back up, squinting at the overly

bright screen. "Well, up yours, Jackson. He wants *your* phone number?"

"What? Mine? Why?"

"For the other guy at the bar. Want me to send it to him?"

"Jasper? Sure." I try to hide the smile from my voice.

Emeryn turns toward me. "Is there something you need to share, Celeste?"

This time, I can't hide the smile. "No. He was just a nice guy. That's all."

She grunts, sliding out of bed. "Don't fall for the first dude that catches your eye. There will be plenty around here, trust me. You're young. Spread your wings and fly." She burps loudly. "I'm heading to the showers." She departs after her words of wisdom.

By the time I shower and dress, there are only thirty minutes before my first class. Emeryn and I head across the traffic circle to the cafeteria. She fills her plate with enough food for both of us, and we sit in the back, where Drake finds us quickly.

"Hi, I'm Drake," he says, setting his tray next to mine. He holds his hand toward Emeryn, who ignores it.

"This is my roommate, Emeryn," I answer for her.

"Ah, the illustrious roommate. It looks like you're feeling better today."

She takes a huge bite of eggs. "Are you always this boring?"

Drake smiles while stuffing his napkin in his collar.

"No. Sometimes I'm a daredevil and don't do my homework until five minutes before class."

"Wow, you are a rebel."

They eat, and I move the food around on my plate quickly. Together, we head to English.

We enter the room with less than a minute to spare, and Oliver doesn't bother looking up. "Who's that?" Emeryn whispers. "He's hot as hell."

"That's Dr. Fitzgerald. Looks can be deceiving." I scoff.

Oliver stands with a smirk on his face.

coding club

THE DAY PASSES QUICKLY. It turns out Emeryn is in most of my classes. I find myself checking my phone throughout the day, hoping for a text, and disappointed when there's nothing there. I follow Emeryn and Drake into the dining hall and do my usual routine of shoving the food around.

"Are you ready for coding club?" Drake asks after clearing his trash.

"That's tonight?"

"Yep." He dramatically pulls his watch in front of his face. "In fifteen minutes."

"What is this club you speak of?" Emeryn asks.

"Coding club. It's computer stuff. Want to come?"

"Wait. Wait. Wait. I couldn't understand your words. All I heard was, nerd, really loudly in my ears."

Drake's eyes grow large. "I'm going to take that as a no?"

She taps his shoulder. "You'd be correct. I have plans with my cell phone in a few minutes. Mama's gonna do some swiping on hot guys. That is if I can find any worth swiping in this Podunk town."

"Ooo...kay," Drake answers. "Celeste, are you ready?"

"Sure." I follow him inside the main building, and instead of going upstairs, we pass through a door that leads to a set of stairs I didn't even know were there. We head down two flights that empty into a dark hallway. "Are you bringing me down here to kill me?"

Drake laughs awkwardly. "No. This was the only place left open to meet." He stops in front of a closed door. "This is it." He knocks on the door in a pattern of short and long combinations of Morse code. The door creaks open, and a small guy with bleached white hair stands in front of it.

"What's the password?"

"Open the door, Donald," Drake says.

"That works. Who is this lovely auburn queen?"

"Celeste," I answer. I look around the room to find five other guys that look similar to Donald. "I'm interested in joining your club."

"Really?" Donald asks. "Are you lost or being forced to be here?" His voice has raised at least an octave.

"Really," I answer. "And I came of my own free will."

Drake leads me across the room to an empty seat that surrounds a round table. "You can sit here."

"What exactly do we do here?"

"We solve world peace and play Dungeons and Dragons," a different guy answers.

Drake scoffs. "Ignore Ivan. We do neither of those things. Usually, we work on creating codes together. Sometimes they're simple. Sometimes they're not. Lately, we've been working on code to control robots."

"We plan on entering a competition in Jackson, next spring."

"That sounds cool. How can I help?"

A blonde guy sets a homemade robot in the middle of the table. He opens an iPad, and the robot comes to life. He slides his fingers on the screen, making the robot move back and forth.

"That's great. What else can it do?"

He slides his fingers around a few more times, and the robot begins turning in a circle, falling halfway through.

"Nothing," the iPad holder answers. "Every time we try to make it do anything besides forward and backward, that happens."

"Can I take a look at the code?" I reach for the iPad.

"We've tried countless times. None of us have been able to get it to work." The nameless kid reluctantly hands me the iPad. "I don't know what makes you think you can do it."

I spend a few minutes reading the already written code and find the error quickly. "May I?"

"Sure," Drake answers.

"Dude, what if she messes something up?" Ivan whispers.

"She's not going to mess anything up. Give her a chance."

It doesn't take long to isolate the issue, and I rewrite the errors. "Here you go." I hand the iPad back to the no-name kid. "Try it."

He scoffs and begins sliding his fingers around. The robot moves back and forth like before, but this time, when it turns in a circle, it completes the job without falling.

"Holy shit. How'd you do that?"

I shrug. "I've spent a good amount of time writing code."

The room cheers. "You just saved us a month's worth of work."

"You're welcome." I slide back in my seat.

"Since we've completed work for the next few meetings, why don't we continue our game?" Donald, the door opener, asks.

"Do you know anything about Star Wars?" Drake asks.

"No. I'm not a big television or movie watcher. I'll leave that conversation for you guys."

Donald starts speaking in a foreign language. I speak over thirty languages, but this one isn't familiar. "Dude, quit speaking Klingon. You know not everyone understands."

That's definitely my cue to leave. I stand, and the

guys around the table wave in unison. "Thanks, Celeste. You're more than welcome to keep coming back."

"Yeah," Donald adds. "We could use your help."

"I'll do that. Thanks." I head toward the door and realize Drake's right behind me.

"I'll walk you back."

"That's not necessary. I'm a big girl."

"Are you sure?"

"Positive. Go explore Star Wars with your friends." I leave the room and head upstairs to the entrance. As soon as I exit the front door, my phone buzzes.

I deliberately don't look at it until I get to the stairs of the dorm. Sitting on the concrete stairs, I take a deep breath before pulling my phone from my pocket.

Hi. Is this Celeste?

My heart leaps into my chest as I try to think of a witty comeback.

Yes

Nailed it.

Who is this?

Jasper. I got your number from your roommate. I hope you don't mind.

No. I don't mind.

Why am I smiling?

WYD?

What does that mean? I'm not good at texting lingo. I do a quick Google search and realize he just asked me what I was doing.

Just got out of a meeting, and heading back to the dorm. What about u?

I smile at my abbreviation of the word you. I'm getting it.

Currently babysitting my older brother. Speaking of babysitting, how's your roomie?

She's doing good. Back to normal. Thanks for your help the other night.

It was my pleasure. I need to go. Jackson's about to get himself in trouble. Text me anytime you're bored. If I don't answer right away, I will when I can.

I guess it's hard to text without opposable thumbs.

He takes a few minutes to respond, and I worry that I've offended him with my sarcasm.

> Nah, I just use my teeth. Good night, vampire.

I laugh out loud, envisioning him typing with his teeth.

> Good night, wolf.

I head upstairs with a smile plastered on my face. "Wow. Was the nerd club that much fun?" Emeryn greets me.

It takes a few minutes for her words to register. "Oh, it was great. I was able to help them do something cool with their robot."

"Now, that does sound interesting."

"Find any good swipes?"

She sighs. "A few. Time will tell if we're a match." She rolls over, facing me. "Speaking of which, spill everything you know about that hot English professor."

"I don't know much. He worked with my dad a few times."

"And?"

"And nothing. That's all I know."

Emeryn smiles. "So, he's free game?"

"He's all yours."

viktor would not approve

THE NEXT MONTH PASSES QUICKLY. Each day is a repeat of the previous, and I've fallen into the routine of college life relatively easily. I haven't seen Jasper since my driving lesson, but we've texted every day. Our texts have evolved from simple "what are you doing" messages to flirty and more frequent, and I'm okay with that.

The clock on my phone alerts me that Emeryn will be waking soon. I slide under the cover, waiting for my alarm to "wake" me. When it goes off, I pretend to stretch and slide out of bed.

"Ugh," she mumbles from across the room. "I don't want to get up."

"Yeah, me neither. I'm heading to the shower." She doesn't respond, but I recognize her feet in the shower next to mine a few minutes later.

Less than an hour later, we're heading toward the

dining hall. "This guy won't take no for an answer," she mumbles, staring at her phone.

"What's going on?"

"This guy I swiped right on. He's been messaging me nonstop for the past week."

I shrug. "Just ignore him."

"I can't. I gave him my phone number."

"You gave who your phone number?" Drake asks, joining us on the walk.

"Why are guys gross, Drake?" Emeryn asks, instead of answering his question.

He stares at me with huge eyes, begging for help. "I...I don't know?"

"Me neither, Drake. Me, neither. Jerk." She stops walking and types something into her phone. I'm scared to know what she just sent. "And blocked." She dramatically pushes a button on her screen.

My phone buzzes in my pocket, and I can't hide the smile that forms. I wait until we're seated at a table before glancing at the message. Instead of a message from Jasper, I'm surprised to see the words on my screen are from Amelia.

> Call me when you can. Found out
> some info from Ollie.

"Excuse me, please. I need to check in with my... friend."

Drake and Emeryn are in a deep conversation about

men, and neither notices when I leave. I head back to the traffic circle and find a remote spot to call.

"*Hello?*" Amelia picks up on the first ring.

"*Hey. What's going on?*"

She laughs. "*It took some convincing, but I got the information out of Ollie.*"

"*Okay, spill.*"

"*Spill? Sounds like you're learning a little bit of college life lingo.*" She pauses. "*Ollie is there for an investigation. Apparently, there have been several students who have disappeared from your school over the past two years.*"

"*Disappeared? What do you mean?*"

"*As in, there one day and gone the next. Ollie thinks there's something supernatural involved. He's there researching.*"

"*So, his being here has nothing to do with me?*"

Amelia laughs again. "*He was as surprised to see you as you were to see him. He's a good guy, Celeste. You can trust him. Viktor trusted him.*"

"*I know. Thank you for researching. What about the Alpha? Did Topher know anything?*"

"*Nothing much. He's met him a few times. His name is Xavier Daniels. From everything Topher said, he sounds like a decent guy, and his pack respects him.*"

I take a deep breath. "*Okay. Thank you, Amelia.*"

"*Anytime. Be careful up there. Maybe you and Ollie can work together.*"

"*I'll think about it.*" I hear her snicker on the other end of the line.

"I've got to go. Let me know if you need anything."

"I will. Bye."

"Bye, sweetie."

"There you are," Drake announces as he and Emeryn exit the dining hall. "Ready for English?"

I plaster a fake smile across my face. "Sure." The three of us head into the main building and up to Oliver's classroom. He smiles, knowingly, when I enter. Dammit, Amelia wasn't discreet.

"I still think he's hot," Emeryn whispers as we take our usual seats in the back of the room.

"Shh, he'll hear you," I whisper.

"Unless he has superhuman hearing, he can't hear me."

I suppress the laugh that forms. If she only knew. Oliver stands and writes the words *Halloween Hoopla* on the board. "Apparently, whether out of spite or revenge, I'm not entirely sure yet, I've been chosen to plan this... event." He points at the board. "It's some sort of school-wide dance, and there's only a week to get the entire thing organized. That's all I've discovered. I am in need of help. Would anyone..."

"Me! I'll help," Emeryn interrupts. "Parties are my thing." Several other girls raise their hands, volunteering their service. Before it's all said and done, Oliver ends up with a list of ten young women who are more than willing to help him with *whatever* he might need.

Emeryn passes me a folded piece of paper with *OMG* written in all caps. Oliver spends the next few minutes giving the class a writing prompt and instructing us to write a three-paragraph short story expanding on the prompt. Writing isn't my strength, and I struggle with the assignment, finishing just as class ends.

My phone buzzes the moment I leave the classroom. Drake and Emeryn both finished their story early, leaving me alone.

GM, Celeste. Wanna hang out?

Yes, I do, but I have three more classes today.

Sure. What time?

I have to work until 4. After that?

That works.

I'll pick u up @ 4:30.

I smile at the thought. We've talked every day, but I haven't seen him since the lake. The rest of the day passes painstakingly slowly. The minute my last class is over, I head straight to the dorm, searching for the perfect outfit. "You've been super smiley all day. What's going on?"

"Nothing," I answer, searching through my closet.

Emeryn steps between me and my clothing choices. "Do I look that dumb?"

"No?"

"Is it Drake?"

"What?" I turn, facing her.

"Do you have a date with Drake?"

I laugh. "Drake is just a friend. There's nothing between the two of us."

Emeryn scoffs. "You might need to let him know that. That boy's so smitten with you. It's written all over his face. "

"Really?" Have I missed that?

"Really," she answers.

I sit on the edge of my bed. "No. It's not Drake. Now I don't know what to do."

"Nothing. You don't do anything. He has a little crush on you. I'm sure it's not the first time someone has fallen in love with that long red hair and those big blue eyes. You're gorgeous. He'd be an idiot not to have a crush on you."

I stare at my roommate, not sure what to say.

"It's Jasper, isn't it?"

I can't hide my smile. "Yes. He's going to pick me up in," I glance at my watch, "twenty minutes. I don't know what to wear."

"Step back. This is my strength." She searches through my clothes, pulling out an overly tight pair of jeans and a fuzzy black sweater. "Wear this with your black knee-high boots."

"Won't that look a little...slutty?"

"That's the point."

I dress quickly and finger pick my curls, bringing them back to life. Sometimes the image in the mirror still catches me by surprise. "How do I look?"

"Like a classy ho," Emeryn answers.

Almost there.

Jasper texts my phone.

Emeryn stuffs a shiny silver package into my bag. "Take this. We don't want any little accidents right now."

"Oh, my God. I'm not planning on sleeping with him."

"Who said anything about sleeping? Go, spread your wings—and legs."

"Emeryn!" She pushes me out the door, closing it behind me.

"Have fun!" she shouts through the closed door.

The walk to the parking lot seems like the longest trip ever. When I finally arrive, I don't see Jasper's truck. Instead, he's leaning against a motorcycle, holding an extra helmet in his hand. "You look... beautiful."

"Thank you. Emeryn dressed me. Where's the truck? I was looking forward to driving."

"I thought I'd switch things up. Are you okay with riding on the back of a motorcycle?"

"That's something I've never done. This is all about

experiencing new things, so yes. Let's do it." Jasper slides the helmet over my head, latching it tightly under my chin. "Where are we going?"

"That's a surprise," he answers, sliding the matching helmet on.

"Should I be worried?"

"Not unless you don't like culture." I climb on top of the bike. He climbs in front of me and between my knees. "Hold on to my sides."

"This is feeling sketchy."

Jasper laughs. "I haven't forgotten you could kill me in a heartbeat."

"Okay, good. The threat still stands."

"I would expect nothing less."

The motorcycle roars to life, and he leaves the parking lot, heading away from Ravenwood. I instantly love everything about this. The freedom I experience from the wind in my face is just what I need. I've spent my entire life being protected and hidden from the world. This is just the opposite. I wrap my arms tight around Jasper's stomach, feeling rock-hard muscles through his thin shirt.

We pass the bar and eventually the entrance to the lake and move into a more populated area. We pass a Natchez City Limits sign, and I realize we're heading into the town that houses my university on its outskirts. He drives us past all the usual offerings, toward the river, parking in a small lot next to a riverwalk. He slides off the bike, helping me down, and puts his helmet on the seat. I copy his movement, not sure what the protocol is for helmet placement.

"Is this the cultural part of our trip?"

"This is it. I present to you, the Mississippi River."

I stare over the familiar water. "Looks pretty much like it does at home."

Jasper laughs. "Yeah, I guess it would. I didn't think that through too well." His hand slides to the small of my back, directing me toward the riverwalk. When he pulls his hand away, I'm surprisingly disappointed.

We move to the railing overlooking the water, and a cool breeze lifts the hair from my shoulders. "Is that a casino?" I point to a paddleboat moving around on the water.

"Yeah. It has to leave land before people can gamble. The open sea is free game."

"It's beautiful. I remember riding on a paddleboat when I was younger."

Jasper turns toward me. "Did you age? I thought vampires stayed the same age they were when they were turned."

I can't control the awkward laugh that escapes. "It's a long story."

"We have time."

"Yes, we do. But I don't know you well enough to share that part of me, yet."

Jasper smiles. "I'm glad you ended that sentence with 'yet.' That means there's hope."

"Don't get pushy, wolf." I nudge him with my elbow, making him laugh.

He leads us to a bench overlooking the river. "I don't get much time alone. When I do, I like to come here. There's something about water that calms me."

"I get that." Feeling bold, I wrap my arm through his and stare over the water. "This is beautiful."

"Yes, you are." I turn, finding him staring at me. "I've never met a vampire before. You're nothing like I expected."

"Still breaking those stereotypes, I see. That was you I saw by the lake that night, wasn't it?"

"I knew I smelled you." His eyes grow. "That didn't come out the way I meant it. You don't stink. I mean, I thought you were there."

I laugh, interrupting his apology. "I know what you meant." I pause, not sure how to say what I want to say. "As a wolf, you were..."

"Scary?" he fills in my words.

"I was thinking more along the lines of beautiful." Jasper slides his hand up, clasping his long fingers around mine. We stare at each other for longer than necessary. I find myself wanting more.

"You're special, Celeste." His eyes glance at my lips, and I fight the urge to turn away.

"Hey, you two," a voice says from behind. "Fancy meeting you here." I turn, seeing the familiar face of Jasper's older brother.

"Jackson? Why are you here?" Jasper asks, letting go of my hand.

"I thought I saw your bike. I didn't mean to interrupt—whatever this is." He looks between the two of us. "Aren't you that chick from the bar?"

I stand, moving toward him. "Celeste." I hold my hand toward him.

"Jackson." He shakes my hand. The energy coming from him is off, but feels nothing like any lycan energy I've experienced before. I don't understand why. It definitely feels lycan but off at the same time. Weird.

"How's that friend of yours? The one with the Porsche?"

Jasper moves in front of me, protectively, and answers for me. "She's doing good. What do you want, big brother?"

"Nothing, *little brother*. I thought you were hanging out alone. I'll let you get back to," he turns back to me, "whatever you were doing. It was nice to see you again, Celeste."

"You too, Jackson."

Jasper's energy has shifted. He watches until Jackson jumps on a motorcycle similar to his and drives away. "I'm sorry about that. He's a bit of an ass."

"I've been around many asses in my lifetime. One more means nothing." I try to lighten the mood.

"Yeah, I would imagine so. Maybe I should get you back."

We walk slowly back to the bike, and Jasper laces

his fingers through mine as we move. He drives slower on the way back to Ravenwood. Several times, his hand brushes my knee, sending goose bumps all over my body. I've never kissed a man before. I'm not sure I even know what to do. Theoretically, I know everything there is to know about sex, but learning from a textbook and learning in person are two different things.

By the time we reach the parking lot, the sun has set, and we're the only two people there. He helps me off the side of the bike. "I don't want to leave," he whispers.

"I don't want you to leave."

He leans down, laying his forehead against mine. "I don't know what to do," he admits.

"You kiss me," I whisper.

One hand slides to my cheek, while the other slowly lifts my chin. His lips gently touch mine, and the sensation that fills me sends chill bumps to every part of my body. His kiss is tentative and exploratory as he shares sweet, tiny kisses with me. I want more. I wrap my arm around his waist, pulling his body tight against mine.

My movements encourage Jasper, and he deepens the kiss, parting my lips with his tongue. I open wide, relishing the feel of his body and mouth against mine. One of his hands slides behind my neck, connecting our bodies all the way down.

I slide my hands under his T-shirt, touching his bare skin, and the heat radiating from him brings more of me to life. A faint howl echoes through the distance.

In an instant, Jasper steps away. "We should stop." He's panting and runs a hand through his already messy hair. "I'm sorry, Celeste." He backs away. "I need to go."

He climbs on the bike, leaving me in the parking lot with swollen lips and uncertainty.

a mission

"YOU'RE HOME EARLY," Emeryn says as I enter our shared room.

"I don't want to talk about it." I plop down on my bed and stare at my blank phone.

"Want to watch a movie then?"

I turn toward her. "Sure. What do you have in mind?"

"What haven't you seen?" she asks, opening her laptop.

"Everything. I've only watched one movie before."

Emeryn closes her laptop and slowly turns her head in my direction. "Are you serious, or did you say that wrong?"

"Nope. I watched *Hotel Transylvania* with my... friend once. That's the only movie I've ever seen." She stares at me blankly.

"This gives me a ton of options. What's your favorite genre?"

"I don't know. Surprise me." She makes her way to my bed, sliding in next to me. "Okay, this is an old one but a good one. By the way, all this pink, touching my skin, is giving me hives."

"You'll live."

Emeryn pushes play. "Is this about vampires?"

"Yes. In honor of Halloween." She giggles.

Almost instantly, her phone starts buzzing. "That's weird," she whispers, answering her text.

"Is something wrong?"

"No. Just a message from a guy. Not one I was expecting to hear from again."

Emeryn spends most of the movie responding to texts and giggling. She's enjoying whoever is texting her. I don't push the issue, but curiosity is about to kill me. When she's ready, she'll tell me. I haven't checked my phone since being back. As badly as I want to talk to Jasper, I'm pissed. I'm sure he heard the howl, which was most likely Jackson. What's his deal?

The movie's over, and Emeryn missed the entire last half, keeping her nose buried in her phone. "It's over."

"Oh, sorry. I was distracted."

"Really? I hadn't noticed."

"You'll never guess who's been messaging me." I raise my eyebrows, waiting for the response. "Jackson. You remember? The guy from the bar."

"Jasper's brother?"

She looks up, surprised. "They're brothers? Oh, my God. How weird is that?"

"Has he been texting you since the bar?"

She laughs. "No. Only one time to ask for your phone number, and then nothing. But he just asked me out."

"Like on a date?"

"No, to fix him dinner. Yes, on a date." Something about Jackson hits me wrong. There's more to the story of Jasper having to watch his older brother. I don't trust Jackson. My phone buzzes for the second time since the movie started. I know without looking that the messages are from Jasper. Reluctantly, I look.

Sorry, I had to run off. I enjoyed
spending time wu.

I hope you're not angry with me.

I drop my phone, refusing to respond. Yes, Jasper, I'm angry with you. I don't understand what happened. Emeryn takes her computer and moves back to the dark side of the room, still giggling at her phone.

"What did you tell him?"

"What?"

"About going out. What did you tell him?"

"I haven't given him an answer yet. I'm keeping him guessing."

I sigh. "What about the guys you've been talking to on Tinder?"

"Duds," she answers. "Nothing compared to this stud."

My phone buzzes again.

> Is Jackson texting your roommate?
> He's acting weird.

He's not the only one, Jasper. I still refuse to answer his texts. I'm feeling rather temperamental tonight.

"Good night, Emeryn." I curl under my covers, hoping she'll go to sleep soon. Much to my chagrin, she doesn't stop texting and finally falls asleep around two o'clock in the morning. I've laid so still that my body feels frozen in place.

Finally, her breathing slows, and I recognize her soft snores. I grab my phone and send a message to Amelia.

> Hey. Can you give me Oliver's phone number?

Several minutes later, she responds with his number and a confused face emoji.

> Don't worry. I just have a question for him.

I send a text to Oliver asking if we can meet. He responds quickly, and we make plans to meet at the benches behind the dorms in ten minutes. I slide out of bed and head to our meeting spot.

"I'm surprised you want anything to do with me," he says from behind.

"Yeah, me too." I turn, facing my English professor. "Why are you here?"

He sighs. "I told you. Me being here has nothing to do with you."

"I understand that. But why are you here? What brought you to Ravenwood in the first place?" Oliver walks around, sitting opposite me on the bench.

"Why do you want to know?"

I rub both hands through my hair. "I don't know. A hunch, maybe?"

"What do you know?"

I scoff. "That's not how this is going to go, Oliver. Why are you here? I may look young, but remember who and what I am." I've never spoken to anyone the way I just talked to Oliver. Internally, I'm shaking. Externally, I'm cool as ice.

"Lycan," he answers.

"What about them?"

"God, you remind me of Viktor." He slides back on the bench. "There has been a rash of missing girls from the area over the past few years. We have reason to believe the wolves are involved."

"Missing?"

"Aye. Four from Ravenwood and two from Natchez." A hint of a foreign accent makes its way to the surface.

"Why am I just now hearing about this?" I cross my arms in front of my chest.

"Because the university has worked hard to keep it quiet."

"Were they found...dead?"

Oliver crosses his legs. "None of them have been found."

"Who is *we*?"

"I'm afraid I don't know what you mean?"

"You said *we* have reason to believe the wolves are involved. Who is we?"

He stands, moving away from the bench. "Much like the groups of vampires that meet at the LaLaurie Mansion, there is a small governing body here. I'm the one who is sent into situations when the need arises. It's why I was sent to New Orleans."

"To investigate the cult?" I fill in the blanks. He nods. "Why do you believe the lycan are involved with these missing girls?"

"Call it a hunch," he repeats my words from earlier.

"Have any students gone missing this semester?"

"No. Whoever is responsible may know that we're on to them. I've tried to lay low, but may have been unsuccessful. Celeste, why do you want to know all of this?"

I sigh. "I'm nosey, I guess."

"I don't buy that for a minute. If you have any information that could help me, please share it." He pauses.

"We have reason to believe these girls are being trafficked."

"Oh, my God. That's horrible."

"I agree. Normally, vampires don't get involved in human situations. This is different. We can't...*I* can't sit idly by and watch. Not when I can stop it from happening to others." He doesn't explain, but I can tell there's more to the reason he's here.

"What if they take me?"

"I don't think you'll be on their radar. If it is the lycan that are involved, they'll know what you are by smell. They're dumb but not that dumb."

I think back to the night in the bar. Neither Jackson nor Jasper knew what I was. Jasper only figured it out when we touched. "What if they don't know me by my smell?"

"Then they're dumber than I thought."

"I'm serious, Oliver. I can help."

He laughs awkwardly. "Your father would come back from his grave to kill me if I even considered letting you be involved with this. Thank you for your concern, but that's not going to happen." He holds his hands in front of his face. "Don't even think about threatening me. I know precisely how old you are and what you're capable of. That has nothing to do with me telling you no."

"Then why?"

"There are many reasons, but the most obvious one is Amelia. In case you've forgotten, your creation has the ability to shift into a wolf at will. She's a vampire-wolf hybrid, and she's dangerous. To be honest, she scares the shit out of me."

I laugh at his admission. "If you won't let me get taken, then at least let me help. I came to college to live and have a life, but to be honest, I'm bored. A little mystery is just what I need."

"Agreed. If I have any need of your services on campus, I will ask."

I smile. "Thank you, Dr. Fitzgerald."

"You're welcome, Miss Luquire. I do believe it's time for you to return to your dorm. If you hear of anything that might be beneficial, let me know immediately."

"So, I'm like a detective?"

"Sure," he answers with a smile. "I need you to be cautious. This isn't a game. If the lycan are involved, they're not the ones in charge. This goes higher than locally."

"I understand, and I'll be careful."

"Goodnight, Celeste."

"Goodnight, Oliver."

I feel his energy watching over me until I'm back inside the dorm. My phone buzzes, grabbing my attention. After asking if Jackson was texting Emeryn, he sent one last text, telling me he would be at the lake all night, alone, if I wanted to talk. Do I want to talk? Maybe he knows something about the disappearances.

On my way.

jackson—a ticking time bomb

I MAKE it to the lake seconds later. Vampire speed is useful. Jasper's truck is parked in the same spot as when I drove us here. The tailgate is down, and he's sitting in the back, staring into the night sky.

I move so softly that no one, human or supernatural, could hear me approach. I fight the urge to jump on him and scare the shit out of him. Instead, I choose a more traumatic version. "Hello, Jasper," I whisper, inches from his ear.

He jumps off the bed of the truck, landing flat on his back on the ground in front of him. He stands quickly and clears his throat. "Celeste. You scared me."

"Good." He slides back on the tailgate, patting a spot next to him. "I'd rather stand, thank you."

"I want to apologize for running off earlier." I don't respond. Instead, I stare blankly at the lycanthrope, not sure what to say or do. He looks at his knees, clearly feeling awkward, and sighs. "Jackson didn't just accidentally show up at the same place we were at. He was following us...following me."

"Why?"

"God, I've never talked to anyone about this before. I'm not sure where to start."

"You can start with why he would be following you."

Jasper stands, moving to the opposite side of the truck. "Jackson has a few *issues*."

"What kind of issues?" I interrupt.

"Ever since he was a kid, he looked at things differently than everyone else. We're Irish twins, only ten months apart, so we've been together our entire lives." He scratches his head, messing up his hair. "When we were kids, he would attack me for the simplest things, taking a toy he was using, or choosing a particular color of crayon that he wanted. Not normal sibling fights, but to-the-brink-of-killing-me fights. One time," he pauses, "one time, he put me in the hospital for a week with a broken nose, a concussion, and a broken femur. All because I ate the last chocolate chip cookie."

"That's not normal," I add.

"Yeah, I know. My parents tried to get him help, but nothing worked. He spent months in psychiatric hospitals, drugged to the point of being a zombie, yet nothing changed his outbursts or behavior. Doctors could never decide on an official diagnosis."

"Not everything has a diagnosis."

He scoffs. "When he shifted the first time...he nearly killed our sister. She tried to help him, but he was out of control. He scarred her for life, and she'll never be the same, mentally, or physically."

"That's why you *watch* him?"

"Yeah. I'm his babysitter."

"That kind of sucks, doesn't it? How did that burden fall on you?"

He pauses. "Because I'm the only one he'll listen to."

"What about your father? Isn't Jackson required to listen to the Alpha?"

"My father only puts up with him. In my opinion, he'd rather him be dead."

For the first time, I soften my stance. "Your father wants his son dead?"

"He's never come right out and said that, but yes. Life without Jackson would be much simpler."

"Isn't he bound to be the next Alpha?"

"Yes. Hence my babysitting duty. My job is to keep him from embarrassing the family any more than he already has and to keep him alive long enough to take over his duties when the time comes."

"That doesn't explain why he was following you."

He sighs. "He's developed an...unnatural attachment to me. He thinks he can't function if I'm not nearby. When I try to get away, he finds me."

"Is he around now?"

"No. Our younger brother is on duty tonight.

Jackson was texting some girl and seemed occupied for the moment. I took the chance to escape for a while."

I shift from one foot to the other. "Yeah, he was texting Emeryn."

"Shit. I knew it. Why didn't you tell me?"

"Do you really need an answer to that?" I cross my arms again.

"Yeah, I'm sorry, Celeste. That was a jerk move. I just didn't want to take the chance of him trying something with you."

"What do you mean?"

"Any girl I've ever tried to date, he somehow interferes with. I didn't want him to know about you."

"He can't hurt me," I remind him.

"I know. But I didn't want to give him the opportunity to try." He slides back on the tailgate.

"Do I need to be worried for Emeryn?" I ask, thinking about my love smitten roommate.

"I don't think so. He's never hurt anyone outside our family. With girls, he just uses them and dumps them all within the same week."

"Jackson sounds like a lovely individual."

Jasper scoffs. "Deep down he's a good guy. He doesn't mean to do the things he does. It's like someone else takes over his body and he's shoved into the background."

"You sound like an abused girlfriend making excuses for her narcissistic boyfriend."

He doesn't speak for a few minutes. "Thank you for coming. I'm sorry I had to leave earlier. Jackson was…"

"I heard him. He was calling you, wasn't he?"

"Yeah."

"What happens if you don't answer?"

He shrugs. "I don't want to find out."

Against my better judgment, I slide beside him on the tailgate, leaving space between the two of us. "I enjoyed our time together. I'll admit, I was confused and angry when you left." I pull my knee beside me and turn toward him. "You don't have to protect me, Jasper. I'm an ancient vampire who's stronger than the majority of vampires in the U.S. I can take care of myself."

"I'm not going to lie. That's hot."

"The thought of me being able to destroy an entire town in minutes is hot?" I can't hide the smile on my face.

"Maybe not that part. You're pretty incredible, Celeste. You, the girl who goes to college just to experience something human. The girl who's been around since medieval times but doesn't know how to drive. That's what's hot."

"You're not getting in my pants."

He holds his hands up. "I can't say it hasn't entered my mind a few hundred times, but I would never belittle you that way."

"Good, because it's not happening. Not to change

the subject or anything, but do you know anything about missing girls from the area?"

"Missing, as in kidnapped?"

"Something like that. I've run across some information about six young ladies who have disappeared from this area."

Jasper shakes his head. "No. I don't watch the news much."

"Have you heard anything from the wolves?"

"Do you think something is going on?"

I shrug. "I'm not sure. I'm thinking about looking into it."

"Let me know if I can help."

The crow of a rooster, miles away, catches my attention. "I need to get back before Emeryn wakes up."

"Yeah, I should do the same before Jackson wakes up or notices I'm missing." He jumps off the tailgate and steps in front of me. "Thank you, Celeste. Thank you for meeting me here and for our short time together earlier. I enjoy every minute with you."

I slide down, putting only inches between the two of us. "I enjoy spending time with you. However, if you want to spend more time together, I have a few conditions."

"Name them," he answers.

"Number one, Jackson cannot get between us."

He nods. "Done."

"Number two, don't ever forget what I'm capable of."

He smiles, raising one side of his mouth higher than the other. "I like living on the edge."

"I'm serious, Jasper."

"I'm not going to forget. I have no qualms about you being more powerful than me. I'm good with that." His eyes slide down to my mouth. "Can I kiss you?"

As much as I want to say yes, I step backward. "No. I'm still pissed." I take off, leaving Jasper standing by the lake and, hopefully, just as confused as I was earlier.

The sun is just starting to glow as I step back into my room and climb under the covers. Emeryn stirs moments later, grabbing her phone. She sighs, setting it down heavily. "Celeste," she whispers loudly.

"Hmm?"

"Are you awake?"

"Yes. Are you?"

Emeryn laughs. "No. I'm talking in my sleep. Can I tell you about my date?"

"Sure," I answer, trying to sound enthusiastic. She jumps out of her bed and onto mine.

"We're going to a restaurant in town, and then he's taking me to meet his family."

I turn toward my roommate. "His family?"

"Yeah! I'm so excited."

"Emeryn, don't you think he's moving a little too quickly? He didn't even start texting you until last night. Now you're going to meet his family."

"I thought you'd be happy for me. Not a stick in the mud." She gets up, moving back to her bed.

"I *am* happy for you. It just seems a little sudden. Did he say why he hasn't contacted you since the bar?"

"No, but I didn't ask. You know how guys are. They do things on their own terms."

I laugh. "No. I don't know how guys are, but I do know you deserve the best. Don't let him treat you otherwise."

"That was kind of nice." She throws a small pillow at my head, which I easily duck away from. "I'll be careful. Don't worry."

"So, when does this date occur?"

"Tonight!"

We take our time getting ready for class. Neither of us is in a hurry. Drake is in his usual spot at the bottom of the stairs as we exit the hallway and head down. Our routine has been the same since the beginning of school. We cross the traffic circle, heading toward the dining hall. "What's new with you guys?" Drake asks, following us inside.

"I have a date," Emeryn answers.

Drake looks up. "Really? With who?"

She shrugs. "Some guy I met at a bar."

"You went to a bar without me?" he asks, looking between the two of us.

"We did. You wouldn't have enjoyed it."

"I'll be the judge of that."

After breakfast, we head upstairs to English. Oliver looks up as we enter. "Good morning," he greets the three of us. "Don't forget our first

Halloween Hoopla meeting is this evening in the dining hall."

"Oh, shit," Emeryn whispers. "I can't be in both places at the same time."

I sigh. "I'll take your place on the Hoopla committee."

She hugs me quickly. "Yay! Thank you, Celeste." The rest of the day passes quickly, and I'm grateful. As a vampire, I have overly sensitive hearing. Over the years, I've learned to ignore sounds and conversations that have nothing to do with me. Today, I've listened to everything and everyone. Other than a few interesting gossip conversations, I've heard nothing out of the ordinary.

Back in our room, Emeryn is dressed and ready for her date. "How do I look?"

I stare at my friend, who's wearing a solid black dress that shows every curve on her body, leaving nothing to the imagination. "You look—amazing."

She slides on a pair of bright red heels and heads toward the door. "Thank you for doing the thing with Dr. Fitzgerald. I would have totally gone and flirted with him, otherwise."

I smile. "I know you would've. I'll let you know what happens. Is Jackson picking you up?"

Emeryn giggles. "On a motorcycle! Eek...I'm so excited."

"Please be careful. If you need anything, a ride home, a friend, anything. I'm one call away."

She laughs. "You act like I'm going out with an animal. It's just Jackson." She closes the door behind her, and I laugh at the irony.

My phone buzzes the moment she leaves the room. I expect to see texts from Jasper, but to my surprise, it's from Oliver.

A student is missing.

From Ravenwood? Who?

A junior. Her name is Autumn Ortega. She's been missing for two days.

Are there any clues?

No. She left for work in town and never returned. Her roommate hasn't heard from her since.

Do you think she's number seven?

There's no evidence to say otherwise. Be safe, and let me know if you hear of anything.

emeryn's date from hell

MY WATCH BUZZES, reminding me to head to the dining hall for the Hoopla meeting. With Halloween in four days, I'm not sure what Oliver thinks we can accomplish in the short amount of time remaining, but I'm here.

I'm surprised to find only two other students and Oliver when I get inside. "Is this the entire committee?" I ask the small group.

"I'm afraid so," Oliver answers. "Several had other obligations."

"You realize this dance is in four days?"

He grimaces in my direction. "I'm fully aware when Halloween is. This should be relatively easy." He pulls a laptop from his bag and hooks it to the projector hanging from the ceiling. The lights go off, and I gain an entirely new respect for my vampire English professor.

He's created a full PowerPoint, complete with music and Pinterest boards of his vision.

"This reminds me of the Addams Family," a girl beside me says. I don't know what that means, but the screen in front of me is covered in black flowers and deep purple decorations.

"That was my inspiration," he answers. "I already have all the flowers and decorations ordered. What I need help with is the setup and organization."

"This is going to be fun," another student adds.

"Good." Oliver smiles. "The dance is this Saturday night. We will have only one day to get the gymnasium ready."

"Where is the gym?" I've never set foot inside it.

"In the basement of the main building. There's a back entrance that will be used for that night only," he answers.

"What about food?" the girl next to me asks.

"A local restaurant is catering. They're going to serve finger foods with a Halloween flair."

How has Oliver had time to teach, investigate the missing students, and plan the party of the season at the same time?

"I think I speak for all of us, Dr. Fitzgerald. You've outdone yourself. I'm a junior, and this dance has been a bust every year. This looks great, and I'm excited to help." I study the profile of the girl next to me as she speaks. Her hair is as black as black can be. Her dark brown eyes are wide and topped with beautifully thick eyelashes.

"I'm Celeste," I whisper.

"Isa," she answers. "Isabella, but my friends call me Isa. This is going to be fun." She turns, facing me, and I notice a deep scar from her hairline to her jaw.

"I think so, too." I don't react to her scar.

"Okay, gang. We ride at eight a.m. Saturday." Oliver looks around the room. "I guess you guys are too young to understand that statement." He clears his throat. "We'll get the decorations together during the evenings, and I'll see you in the gym at eight on Saturday morning to set everything up."

We stand, leaving the room. Isa walks beside me. "You're a freshman?"

"Yes, first year in college." Why do I feel so awkward?

"You're going to do great. This is my third year, and I love it here. I'm glad I chose Ravenwood."

"Me, too." I smile. We walk across the circle together. "I've never seen you around. I guess freshmen and juniors don't mix much."

"That, and I don't live on campus." She heads toward the parking lot. "I'll see you Saturday. It was nice to meet you, Celeste."

"Likewise," I answer, realizing I sound old. "You, too. Bye."

I head back upstairs and complete my English homework, along with the work required on the syllabus for the entire year. No doubt, I'm going to regret doing that when I'm bored with nothing to do later in the year. But for now, it's keeping me occupied.

My phone buzzes, and I'm surprised to see that it's already midnight. I haven't heard anything from Emeryn since she left. Remembering my and Jasper's conversation, I decide to send her a text just to check in.

How's it going?

An hour later, she still hasn't responded. Am I being paranoid? Is this what college kids do? Stay out with strange men they don't really know, and ignore their roommate's texts? To be honest, I don't know. I decide to text Jasper.

Hey. Is Jackson around?

Yeah, he's been home since ten.
What's up?

Something's wrong.

Emeryn hasn't returned from their date.

Shit. BRB

It takes one deep dive on the internet to find his home address. I don't wait to hear back from Jasper before finding the location on Google and heading in that direction at vampire speed. I have to stop every few miles to give the GPS time to catch up with me. Two minutes later, I'm standing outside of a modest cottage on the outskirts of Natchez. Parked in front is Jasper's truck, along with several other cars and motorcycles.

The cottage looks like an ordinary home in the country. I would never think that the Alpha Wolf for the area lives here.

I'm outside.

I send a text to Jasper. Minutes later, the front door opens, and a familiar face exits. He stands in the doorway, searching the night.

"Celeste," he whispers.

"Here."

He runs to the tree I'm leaning against. "How'd you find my house?"

"Google."

He smiles, knowingly. "I highly doubt that."

"What did you find out?"

"Nothing. Jackson says he took her back to the university after they ate."

I cross my arms. "Emeryn told me he was bringing her to meet his family."

"Shit. That never happened."

"What did he do with my roommate?" Anger fills my voice.

"Celeste, Jackson's a dick, but he wouldn't hurt Emeryn."

"How do you know?"

He runs a hand through his hair. "He's my brother."

"The same brother you're sworn to babysit until he becomes Alpha."

My phone buzzes with a text from Emeryn.

Hey roomie. Where are you?

"It's Emeryn. She must be back."

Are you okay?

Yeah, I'm good. Y?

No reason. See you soon.

I sigh. "She says she's fine. Are you sure Jackson has been home since ten?"

He shrugs. "After he picked her up, and they went to the restaurant, I came home. He came into our room at pretty much ten o'clock on the dot."

"Then where the hell has Emeryn been for the past three hours?"

"Without trying to sound like an asshole, that sounds like a question for Emeryn."

He's right. "Another girl is missing," I change the subject.

He steps closer. "Really?"

"A junior. Her name is Autumn."

"What does it mean?"

I shrug. "I don't know. My gut tells me it's not good." I kick the dirt in front of me. "I'm sorry I woke you. I feel kind of dumb for jumping to conclusions. After our conversation, I just…"

"You don't owe me an explanation. I would've thought the same." He reaches for my hand, lacing his fingers through mine. "I don't mind middle-of-the-night visits from you. However, any other vampires are not welcome. Especially in the middle of the night."

I smile, gripping his hand. "I'll let the committee know."

"There's a committee?"

I laugh, leaving him standing in place. I'm back at the dorm minutes later, slowing down only as I open the door to the room. Emeryn is sitting on the edge of her bed. "Are you okay?"

She looks up with a smile. "I'm better than great." She flops back on her bed. "I'm in love."

"One night, and you're in love?"

She sighs loudly. "Yes."

"Emeryn, where have you been?"

She stares at me like I'm dumb. "With Jackson…on a date."

"Do you realize what time it is?"

She looks at her phone. "That can't be right. Is it really two o'clock?"

"Yes. Where have you been?"

"I…I don't remember anything after dinner."

"Did you meet his family?" I already know the answer.

She smiles. "I did. I met his brothers. He has four of them. They came to eat with us."

Now I'm confused. Jasper didn't say anything about meeting them for dinner. From the picture I found online, he doesn't have four brothers. "You don't remember anything after that?"

"No, not really. I remember being back here and sending you a text."

"Emeryn, could you have possibly been drugged again?"

She looks confused. "I don't see how."

"Did anything happen between you and Jackson?"

"If you're asking if we had sex, no. We were with his family." Her words become mumbled. "I'm sleepy."

Something's not right, and I have no clue what. Why would Jasper say that Jackson had been home since ten? Is he covering for him? Is Emeryn confused? I don't know the answers, but my gut tells me it has something to do with the missing junior.

> Are you sure you didn't eat with Emeryn and Jackson?

I send a text to Jasper.

> No. I told you the truth. After he picked her up, I left. Y?

She says his family ate with them.

What? That's crazy. No one in my
family ate with them.

Then who the hell did? She has no
memory after dinner, and she's acting
weird.

I'll find out.

let's get ready to party

THE WEEK FLIES BY. Our small committee has met every night and has the table decorations, balloon arch, and flower arrangements completed. All we need to do is load everything into the gym tomorrow morning and decorate.

Emeryn has spent every night this week with Jackson. Thankfully, she's been home by ten o'clock and has been acting like herself. Or at least, the version of her that thinks she's in love.

"Who are you going to the dance with?" Isa asks as we leave the English classroom/hoopla storage center.

I stop walking. "I haven't even thought about bringing a date. Is that what people do?"

Isa laughs. "It's a dance, Celeste. Unless you're planning on dancing with yourself or just not into that sort of thing, people bring dates."

"I have an idea of who to ask. I hope he doesn't have plans already."

"If all else fails, you can take that guy you're always hanging out with."

"Drake?" I laugh. "We're just friends."

She scoffs. "You might want to let him know that."

I turn toward my new friend. She's the second person that's mentioned that to me. Maybe I should talk to him. Isa turns toward the parking lot, and I head upstairs to check on my roommate. She should be home by now, at least, I hope.

"Hey, roomie," Emeryn greets me as I enter our shared room.

"Hey. You're home early."

"Yeah, we didn't do anything tonight. He had some family thing to do."

I plop on my bed. "Are you bringing Jackson to the dance tomorrow night?"

Her face turns pouty. "I asked him, but he hasn't given me a final answer. However, we both know how convincing I can be." She wiggles her eyebrows with her words. "What about Jasper?"

"I haven't asked," I admit.

Emeryn sits up. "Girl, why not?"

"To be honest, I haven't thought about it. I've never been to a dance before. What are you wearing?"

That's a call to arms for her. She jumps from her bed and heads straight to my closet. "Well, it's a Halloween dance, so you don't need to show up in pink." She flips through my entire wardrobe, pulling out four suitable choices. "Choose one of these." She hangs the choices on the outside of the closet, facing forward.

In front of me are three dresses and a pantsuit. I grab the pantsuit from the ledge, handing it to her.

"Wise choice, my friend. Add a pair of strappy sandals with this, and you'll slay the night."

"Is that what I want to do? Slay?"

"Yep. Go ask that guy to go with you. If not, I'm sure Drake is chomping at the bit."

"Am I completely missing something with Drake?"

"You'd have to be blind and clueless not to see how much he likes you. He stares at you with puppy-dog eyes." Her arms slide across her chest. "You seriously haven't noticed?"

"How do I let him know I'm not interested in him like that? He's a friend, and I want it to stay that way. I don't want to hurt his feelings."

"Then don't say anything about it. When he sees you're with Jasper, he'll move on. It's the way of the world. The circle of life, if you will."

"That seems cruel." The thought of hurting Drake makes me sad.

"Nah, he'll be fine. If you don't text Jasper, I'm going to do it for you." Emeryn points at my bed. "Sit. Text. Now."

I plop on my bed and grab my phone. "Yes, ma'am."

Hey, are you awake?

I am. We're at a pack meeting. So
boring.

That's the family thing.

Are you busy tomorrow night?

Celeste, are you asking me out?

Maybe. How do you feel about
dances?

As in dancing?

I send a laughing emoji.

As in, coming to Ravenwood and
attending the Halloween Hoopla
with me.

I'd be honored.

I can't hide the smile that covers my face. "I'm
guessing he said, yes?" Emeryn asks. "From the look on
your face, you're not sad."

"He said, Yes."

Good. It's at seven o'clock. I'll meet
you in the parking lot around then.

Sounds perfect. Thank you for the
invitation.

Several minutes pass with neither one of us texting. He sends one last text.

> Looking forward to dancing the night away with you.

I feel the pink covering my cheeks. "Since I'm filling in for you on this committee, we could use your help in the morning, getting everything ready."

Emeryn sighs. "Okay. What time?"

"We're meeting at eight."

She climbs under the covers and goes to sleep quickly. I spend the rest of the night reading an entire series of vampire novels I found on Amazon. The author's take on the lives of vampires leaves me both frustrated and in awe of her characters. My phone buzzes again, and butterflies take flight, thinking it's Jasper.

> Remember the rules.

What the hell? I throw my phone on the bed beside me. How can I forget the rules? My entire life rotates around the rules. My mind flashes back to the priestess who issued the warning to begin with. It was immediately after that she changed my life forever. My life had been changed once before, but the moment I killed someone, it went away. Returned to the body of a five-year-old once more. I've spent nearly eight hundred years in that body. I stare into the full-length mirror hanging on the closet door. The woman staring back at me looks nothing like the immortal child I am. Or was… I'm not sure which.

I stand, hoping to change the trajectory of my thoughts. I don't want to think about that night or five-year-old Celeste. I don't want to think about the rules. I want to experience my life the way I want to experience my life. Leave me the hell alone.

"You good?" Emeryn's sleepy voice asks from the other side of the room.

"Bad dream," I lie. I glance at the clock on her night-stand and see that there are only a few hours until eight. "I'm going to take a shower."

The warm water helps clear my mind and brings me back to reality. Pushing that night and the last few years from my mind doesn't help me get over every-thing, but it helps keep me sane.

Emeryn and I enter the English room exactly at eight o'clock. Besides Oliver, we're the first ones here.

"Good morning, ladies. Today is the day! I'm feeling positive about the final outcome this evening."

Emeryn saunters closer to Oliver. "Is there anything else I can do to help?"

He steps back a few steps. "No, thank you, Emeryn. I think we have everything taken care of."

I feel secondhand embarrassment from the other side of the room. Thankfully, Isa and the girl whose name I haven't caught enter, saving Emeryn from herself.

"Good morning, Isa. Good morning, Stephanie. Are we ready to get started?" Oliver announces, moving away from Emeryn.

Stephanie...that's her name. The girls smile as the five of us begin loading our premade decorations into the rolling cart Oliver magically pulled from a closet. We load the elevator and head down four floors to the basement. The door slides open, revealing a huge, empty room.

"This is the room we're decorating?"

"Yep," Oliver answers. "As you can see, we have a bit of work to do."

"That's an understatement," Emeryn mumbles.

Oliver begins spouting orders from a notebook he pulled out of nowhere. I'm grateful he's organized because this feels completely overwhelming. We begin by pulling round tables from a closet next to the stage and setting them in the middle of the floor. In just a few short hours, we have enough tables and chairs out to seat everyone with tickets.

Emeryn and I have made countless trips back to the classroom and have all of the table decor delivered to the gym. "Celeste, can you, Isa, and Emeryn decorate the tables and get them ready for tonight? Stephanie, you and I are going to work on the catering table."

"We're having it catered?" Emeryn asks. "Why did I expect Rotel cheese dip and tortilla chips?"

"I don't know what that is, but aye, we're having a fully catered meal," Oliver makes a face with his words.

"Excuse me, Dr. Bougie," she answers, making me laugh.

The five of us manage to transform the gym into a Halloween party with a few hours to spare. I step back, admiring the room and Oliver's planning ability. "This looks great, Dr. Fitzgerald," Isa yells from across the room.

"It does. We make a good team," he answers.

This is exactly what I envisioned when I decided to go to college. If this doesn't scream human experience, nothing does. My first dance ever is tonight!

"Thank you, ladies." Oliver looks at his watch. "We have two hours before the food arrives and three hours before students will begin arriving. I think I can handle it from here. Tonight, you're not on duty. Enjoy yourself, and I'll worry about cleanup."

The girls head toward the elevator with whispers of "thank you," escaping their lips.

"You coming?" Emeryn asks from the door.

"I'll be there in a minute. I want to ask Dr. Fitzgerald about an assignment."

She shrugs and loads the elevator with Isa and Stephanie. I wait for the doors to close and their voices to become faint before speaking. "There will be two lycan at the dance tonight."

Oliver turns toward me. "They are quite prolific. How do you know this?"

I shift from foot to foot. "They're brothers. Jackson is Emeryn's date, and Jasper is mine."

He moves a large vase of black roses from one table to another. "I don't see an issue with that. I have nothing against the wolves."

"Do you still think they're involved in the disappearances?"

He turns to face me. "To be honest, I don't know who is involved. Every clue seems to lead to a dead end."

"What about the missing girl from here? Any news on her?"

"No. No clues, no nothing."

"There have to be clues. We just need to find them."

He claps his hands together. "Tonight, we focus on this Hoopla." He looks around the room. "This turned out better than I expected. Go get ready, and bring that wolf. Maybe you can teach him to dance. Most of them are all feet and fur."

the hoopla that is halloween

"YOU LOOK HOT," Emeryn announces as we exit the dorm. "That pantsuit, in contrast with your bright red hair, makes you look like a creature of the night." She sticks her teeth on top of her lip.

"A what?"

She laughs. "You know. A vampire."

"Yeah, that's funny." I fight to keep my face even as we walk to the parking lot together. True to her promise, Emeryn convinced Jackson to come, and the brothers are planning on riding together.

"You look beautiful," I tell her as we walk. She chose a pair of high-waisted purple velvet pants and a black ruffly blouse. The price of her clothes seems to match the price of her car. Her coal black hair is pulled into a tight low bun, accentuating her dark eyes. She looks like she belongs on a runway, not at college.

"Thank you. I feel beautiful." I hear the sound of Jasper's truck as they're approaching the school.

"They're almost here."

"How do you know? Did Jasper text you?"

Luckily, I don't have to answer. His truck pulls into the parking lot, stopping at the closest spot to where we're standing. Emeryn runs to the parked truck, grabs the passenger door, and throws herself at Jackson. I decide to play it cool and wait for Jasper to come to me.

He moves in front of me with his hand behind his back. "You look...breathtaking."

I look down before speaking. No one besides my father has ever given me compliments. It feels strange. "Thank you. So do you."

He's wearing a pair of pleated black pants with sharp creases down the front. His navy-blue button-down shirt is tucked in smoothly, making him look like he stepped out of a magazine. "Thank you. I took a bath." He hands me a box with a black and red corsage inside. "I got this for you. I thought the colors were kind of fitting."

"Thank you." I open the box, and he slides the corsage onto my wrist. "It's perfect."

"I didn't get you one of those dumb things," Jackson announces to Emeryn.

"That's okay. I wouldn't have wanted one anyway." They laugh, leaving us in the parking lot alone.

"Looks like I chose wisely," I whisper for Jasper's ears only.

"Shall we?" He holds his elbow toward me, and I lace my arm through. "So, this is what college looks like, huh?"

I laugh. "I don't think this is a true representation. This is a small fine arts college in rural Mississippi. If you want to experience real college life, you'd have to go to one of the big state schools."

"College is not in my future."

"Does that upset you?" I turn toward my date for the night.

He scrunches his face. "It used to but now, not so much. It is what it is."

"This is the first dance I've ever been to." I change the subject.

He stops walking. "Seriously? You never went to any dances in high school."

I start moving. "I never went to high school. I've been homeschooled my entire life."

"If my mother tried to homeschool me, I would've ended up buried in the backyard somewhere. She's not the teacher type."

"Different nannies helped throughout the years. As I aged mentally, they didn't need to help me any longer." I don't elaborate as we enter the basement gym door.

Several students are standing in the foyer, blocking the entrance into the actual gym. Most of them are members of the coding club and smile as we pass. Ivan touches my arm. "Damn, Celeste. You look hot tonight."

Jasper clears his throat, and Ivan steps back a few feet. "Ivan, this is my date, Jasper."

"It's nice to meet you, Jasper."

"Why are you out here in the hall? The party is inside," I ask, hoping to ease the tension.

He knocks into the shoulder of the guy next to him. "This is where the cool kids are."

"Okay. Well, we're going in. Guess we're not cool."

"That was strange," Jasper whispers.

"Yeah. They're super smart, but not good at socializing."

He laughs. "I'd have never guessed." The gym is full as we enter, and I'm glad to see the students participating in the activity we worked so hard to pull together.

The catering table is full of different types of meats, cheeses, and hors d'oeuvres of every kind. A live band has set up on the small stage at the side of the room, and the designated dance floor is full of people moving to the beat.

"Wow," Jasper whispers as we enter. "This looks just like I imagined it would."

"Thank you. I helped decorate." I lead him to a table off to the side. "Are you hungry? You can grab something to eat."

He pulls a chair out and directs me into it. "I'll be right back. You'll be okay on your own?"

"Are you seriously asking me that question?"

"Sorry. Temporary moment of insanity." He laughs. "I'll be right back."

"Hey, Celeste. You look beautiful." I look up to see Darby, my friend from Biology.

She's wearing a simple green dress that hugs her hips. "So do you."

"Dr. Fitzgerald outdid himself. The gym looks great."

Jasper returns, carrying two plates and two cups. "Hi," he greets Darby. "I'm Jasper."

She looks him up and down. "I'm Darby. Are you Celeste's date?"

"Yes? At least, I think I am." He flashes a toothy grin.

"I'll see you later, Celeste." I watch her walk away, not sure what that was about.

"That was weird." Jasper sets a plate in front of me. "I know you don't eat, but I thought you might want to pretend."

"Thank you. I'm good at pushing food around on the plate."

I enjoy people watching, while Jasper cleans both of our plates. Jackson and Emeryn are in the middle of the dance floor, making a scene. Everyone's eyes are on them as they dance like they're from a movie. Oliver was wrong. Some lycan can dance. I laugh to myself.

"What?" Jasper asks.

"Nothing."

He stands, holding his hand out to me. "Would you like to dance?"

"I...I don't really know any modern dances."

"What dances do you know?"

I slide back in my chair. "Daddy taught me the branle and the waltz."

Jasper smiles, lifting one side of his mouth higher than the other. This is the second time he's flashed a crooked smile at me, and I like it. "I don't even know what the branle is, but something tells me it wouldn't go over well on this dance floor. How about you let me lead?"

"I think that would be for the best." I follow him to the floor. The moment we get there, the band changes songs and shifts to a slower tempo. "May I?" he asks, placing his hand on my waist.

"You may." He takes my other hand into his, pulling me closer. "What dance are we doing?"

"It's called the get as close as you can dance." Jasper pulls me so close, there's barely any space between us.

"You smell nice," I whisper.

"Thank you. It's A negative."

I burst out laughing, drawing attention from everyone in the room. "That's not what I meant. You smell like a mixture of pine and dirt."

"Wow. I think I'd prefer you smell my blood. I took a shower and everything."

The top of my head barely comes to his chin. He leans down, resting his forehead on the top of my head. "I could do this all night."

In a moment of complete bravery, I look up, meeting his eyes. "Only this?"

His pupils dilate with my words. I've never really kissed a man before. Our kiss before was interrupted, and left me wanting more. This is my moment to live a life that I was denied for so long.

I don't wait for him to make the first move. I reach up, touching his lips with mine. He doesn't hesitate to return the kiss, claiming my mouth with his. I want more of him. I pull him closer and sigh as our tongues touch.

"Ouch," Jasper pulls away, holding his lip.

"Oh, my God. Did I bite you?"

He pulls a handkerchief out of his pocket, wiping the small amount of blood away. "I'm fine." He holds the cloth in front of me. "See, only a little dot."

"I'm so sorry, Jasper."

He grabs my arms, pulling me in close. "Celeste. I'm fine. You didn't hurt me."

"What if I had drunk from you?"

"You didn't. In fact, it was kind of hot." He closes the space between us. "I'm an easy bleeder."

I scoff. "Then you're here with the wrong girl."

The song ends, transitioning into something with a faster beat. The dance floor erupts into a choreographed dance that everyone except me seems to know. "Come on, it's easy." Jasper drags me further into the floor, and we begin moving with everyone else. He's right. In minutes, I have the steps learned and am following along like an expert. When the song ends, everyone erupts in applause.

"There's someone I want you to meet." I drag him toward my English professor, who's nursing a mocktail and standing in the back corner by the stage. "Dr. Fitzgerald, I'd like you to meet my date, Jasper."

Oliver holds out his hand. "Welcome, Jasper. It's always a pleasure to see a lycanthrope who isn't trying to destroy the building."

Jasper's eyes grow large. "Oliver's like me," I whisper.

"Oh. I really need to work on my ability to recognize vampires." He takes a relieved breath. "It's a pleasure to meet you, Dr. Fitzgerald."

"I do hope you're enjoying yourself, Celeste."

"I am. Thank you."

He turns back to Jasper. "Your brother has managed to sneak in a little alcohol."

"Seriously? I'm sorry about that. I'll get him, and we'll go."

"That's not necessary. I'm watching him. Enjoy yourselves." Oliver pats Jasper on the arm.

"I knew he'd do something stupid. He promised to behave tonight." He waits until we're away from Oliver to complain.

"Oliver will keep him in check."

"Did you know him before you came here?" He nods toward Oliver.

"I did. We never hung out together, but he spent some time with my father."

"He's a teacher?"

I shrug. "I think he fills in when he's needed or investigating."

"He's here investigating the missing girls?"

Someone taps me on the shoulder. I turn to find Drake. He's wearing a three-piece black suit with a bright orange bow tie. Even for Drake, his clothing choice is a bit strange. "Hey, Drake. You clean up pretty well," I lie.

"Thanks. Want to dance?"

I turn back toward Jasper. "I'm on a date."

Jasper waves. "It's fine." He steps up, offering his hand to Drake. "I'm Jasper."

"Drake." I watch as they shake hands. "I'd like to dance with my friend."

"Sounds good, man. It'll give me time to grab more food."

Drake takes my hand and leads me to the dance floor. "I need to warn you. I'm not a very good dancer."

"That's not what I saw earlier."

I stop moving. "You were watching me?"

"How could I not? Look what you're wearing."

I step back from my friend. "Drake, what's going on?"

"I thought you were different from the others. But seeing you like this, I realize you're all the same."

"That's enough. I don't know what's going on, but I'm done dancing."

"Why? So, you can go back to that poor excuse for a man over there? You're a slut like the rest of them."

"Drake. I need you to stop. You're not acting like yourself."

He grabs my hand, trying to pull me to the side of the room. I don't fight and let him take me to the cinderblock wall. "Why are you with him, Celeste?"

"I'm with Jasper because I like him."

"He's a wolf, Celeste." Every alarm in my body goes off in unison. This isn't the Drake I know.

"What do you mean?"

"He's a werewolf. They're dumb and beneath you."

"Why would you think he's a wolf?"

"Quit playing stupid. We both know you're not. I know what he is, and I know what you are."

"I'm leaving."

He grabs my arm, pulling me back. He's stronger than I expected. "Take this warning before you go." He puts his mouth next to my ear. "Don't. Forget. The. Rules."

I step back, staring at the man I thought was my friend. "Who are you?"

He turns, disappearing into the crowd.

the deal of a lifetime—literally

JASPER'S at my side in an instant. "What's going on? I saw your friend stomp off."

"My *friend* is not who I thought he was."

"Do you want me to talk to him?"

"No. I need some fresh air." Jasper follows me out of the gym, past the welcoming committee to the tables behind the dorm.

I sit on one of the benches and take a deep breath. "Celeste. You can tell me what's going on. I told you my life story practically the first night we met."

"Jasper, what I need to tell you is something only a handful of people on Earth know." I stand, walking away from him.

He's at my back quickly. "I'm not going to tell anyone."

I turn, facing him. "If anyone were to find out, I

would have to take care of them and you. Do you understand what I'm saying?"

His eyes search mine. "Yes."

I lace my fingers through his, leading him to the bench. "I'm not what you think I am."

"I know who…"

"No. Please don't try to help. I need you to listen."

He nods. "When I was made a vampire, I was five years old." I look at him. "Do you know what that means?"

"You were a child?"

"Yes. I stayed a child for nearly eight hundred years." I give him a minute to digest my words.

"But…"

"I was called an immortal child, and I was a forbidden life. Even vampires have rules that are not crossed." To his credit, he doesn't interrupt. "For that reason, my father kept me hidden. I was given the best of everything and the freedom to do whatever I wanted, as long as I didn't leave the house." I wring my hands together at the memories. "Through the centuries, I've studied art with Van Gogh, taken piano lessons from Beethoven, and studied science with Da Vinci."

Jasper's eyes grow large.

"None of it compared to having a life of my own. I was a prisoner of my childhood for all of those years."

He reaches over, taking my hand into his. "I'm not seeking your sympathy, Jasper. I need to tell you this. Hell, I need to tell someone."

I take a deep breath before continuing. "I discovered there were people in this world with the ability to *change* what I was—to help me become something other than an immortal child. I pursued many practitioners before finally settling on one I could trust. It took several years and more money than I should mention, but it worked. The process was painful and nearly killed me, but I survived, and my body grew. I became this." I run my hand down my body. "When I was changed, several rules were given to me. One of them was to agree never to take a life. I agreed without hesitation. The only lives I had ever taken were strigoi. With their threat gone, I didn't have any qualms about agreeing with the conditions."

He grasps my hand tighter. "The night my father… died, I broke that rule. I murdered the creature that killed him, and I was instantly changed back into the body of a five-year-old." I wipe the tears streaming down my face. "The creature not only killed my father, but she was going to kill my creation. The only vampire I've ever made."

Jasper looks confused but doesn't interrupt.

"You're wondering how I'm in this body?" I take in a deep breath. "A year passed, and I hid. Remember, I said immortal children are forbidden?"

He nods.

"When I transformed back into a child, I ran and stayed hidden from the ones who would want me dead. During that time, I searched for another practitioner.

Someone who could help me not be a child any longer." I look into his eyes. "I found the person I was seeking. This time, there were new rules and new conditions."

"What are the rules?"

I take a deep breath before answering. Do I share this information with him? His eyes stare back at me with sincerity and trust, making me do something I've never done before. Share my deepest, darkest secret.

"I will never stop aging. I will no longer be in the body of a five-year-old, but unlike all other vampires, I will grow old and eventually die."

"What does that mean?"

"It means I will live the average life span of a human, unless..."

"Unless what?"

"Unless I take another life."

"If you take a life, you transform back into this... immortal child?"

"Yes. I'll be trapped in the body of a five-year-old forever."

Jasper stands. "What the hell kind of choice is that?"

"It was the one I agreed to. I'd rather live and grow old than be a child any longer."

"That won't be hard. Just don't kill anyone. You're one of the calmest people I know. You're not going to kill anyone."

"I'm a vampire, Jasper. Not only that, I'm an immortal child vampire. I once killed twenty strigoi without breaking a sweat. It's why we're forbidden. Immortal children are unpredictable, and most are out of control."

"That's not you."

"No, but it can be."

Jasper picks a large curl, running it through his fingers. "I'll make sure you don't get put in that position."

I take his hand into mine. "Jasper, I appreciate the sentiment, but there's no way you can do that. I am and will always be a vampire."

"What are you two doing out here?" Emeryn giggles as she and Jackson walk up behind us. "We thought we'd be out here alone."

I stand, wiping any residual tears from my cheeks. "We came out to get some fresh air."

"So did we," Jackson's words are slurred as he grabs one of Emeryn's breasts. "If you know what I mean."

"Jackson, you're drunk. It's time to go." Jasper stands, moving closer to his brother.

"I'm not ready to leave," he spews. "I'm about to make Emeryn a woman."

Emeryn scoffs. "That ship sailed years ago."

"Then I'm about to leave my mark." Jackson pushes Jasper away. "Leave me alone, man. I'll come home when I'm ready."

"No. You'll come home now."

A low growl escapes Jackson. "I said, I'll come home when I'm ready. You can tell Dad to go fuck himself and take my little babysitter along for the ride."

"That's enough." Jasper refuses to back down. "You will not speak like that around the ladies."

"Ladies? Have you met Emeryn?"

"Hey," she protests. "I'm a lady." She burps loudly, echoing off the trees that surround us. "See?" She giggles again. She's clearly drunk.

"It's time to go to our room, Emeryn." I move to her side, turning her back toward the dorm.

"Celeste, you're no fun," she protests, but doesn't fight, as I take her upstairs.

"Thank you," Jasper whispers for my ears only. I hear the truck start as we get into the room. Emeryn collapses on her bed and begins snoring before I close the door behind us.

Other than the kiss Jasper and I shared, tonight has been horrible. I've never told my secret to anyone other than Fran. Oliver witnessed what happened the night Viktor died, but no other people know my fate. Telling Jasper goes against everything I believe in. However, telling him lifts a little of the ever-present heaviness from my chest.

I never had the opportunity to tell Jasper about Drake's words. How would he know the rules? Could he be possessed by the voodoo priestess? Could he know her? Questions fly through my mind in rapid succession. None of which I have answers for.

Made it home with Jackson. Sry we
didn't finish talking.

Me 2.

Are you okay?

Am I okay? My go-to answer has always been, "Yes,
I'm fine." Am I fine? Truthfully, I don't know.

I'm good.

I lie.

I take Emeryn's shoes off and pull her blanket on
top of her, before changing into more comfortable
clothes and dragging out my laptop.

Three hours into research, I've only found a small
amount of information on Drake, and that was from an
online version of Ravenwood's yearbook from last year.
Until finding that, I had no clue what his last name was.
I really need to be a better friend. I glance at my snoring
roommate. I don't even know her last name, and we've
shared a room for nearly two months.

Drake's last name is listed as Overstreet. From the
lack of information I've discovered on Drake Overstreet,
I seriously doubt that's his actual last name.

I'm about to give up when I come across an old
death certificate for Drake Alan Overstreet. He was
eighteen years old and died thirty-five years ago in a

boating accident off the coast of Florida. I click through the newspaper clippings until finally finding a picture of the same man I know as my friend. "What the hell?"

He looks the same, but that's not possible. If he had survived, he'd be in his sixties. Unless...

I send a text to Oliver.

> Is Drake a vampire?

He responds quickly.

> Drake? The young man you hang out with?

> Yes. Is he a vampire?

> Not that I'm aware of. We'd both sense him if he were. Why?

> I found an article with his picture that shows he died thirty-five years ago.

> Send it to me. I'll look it over.

I send him the link to the article and continue my search. Finding nothing more on Drake Alan Overstreet, I change the order of his name. This time, searching for Alan Drake Overstreet. I immediately find several mentions with similar spellings. One, in particular, catches my eye. An article from Mobile, Alabama, discusses the death of Alan Drake Overwood, an eighteen-year-old dock worker, who was pulled into the bay and drowned after a rope was accidentally wrapped around his ankle. The article is from the late 1800s, and there are no photographs.

Drake told me he was from Mobile, Alabama. This has to be him. If it is, that means he's over a hundred and thirty years old. I take a screenshot and send it to Oliver.

What does this mean?

He responds quickly.

I have no idea. He knew things he shouldn't know.

About?

Me and the deal I made to be in this body.

We'll talk tomorrow. Keep searching, and I'll do the same.

sunday dinner

"DID YOU STAY UP ALL NIGHT?" Emeryn's sleepy voice asks from across the room.

"I needed to study," I lie. "How do you feel this morning?"

"Like a gorilla and an elephant had a baby, and all three are sitting on my head."

I laugh. "That good, huh?"

"What happened?"

"You and Jackson had your own personal party. You were drunk."

She covers her eyes with her pillow. "How embarrassing." My phone buzzes.

> Would you and Emeryn like to come to my house and officially meet my family?

"Feel like going to Jackson and Jasper's house?"

"Are you serious? For what?"

"To meet their family."

Emeryn sits up quickly. "I already met their other brothers."

I slide off my bed, moving to the edge of hers. "Do you remember anything from that night? I know we already talked about it, but I hoped maybe you would remember something since a few days have passed."

She yawns, stretching her hands high above her head. "No, but I'm not worried about it."

"Emeryn, how could you not be worried about it? You're missing three or four hours of your life."

She shrugs, getting out of bed, making it clear she's finished with that part of the conversation. "What time are we going?"

Sure. What time?

Dinner is served around twelve-thirty.

"He says twelve-thirty," I relay the information to my roommate.

"That gives me time to get presentable."

We'll be there around noon.

Good. I miss you.

His words bring chill bumps to the surface. I've been alive for hundreds of years, but hearing those

141

words from a twenty-year-old lycanthrope makes me feel like a child inside.

We leave the dorm, heading toward the Alpha of North Mississippi's house thirty minutes early. I tried to talk Emeryn into letting me drive, but wasn't able to convince her that Jasper taught me. Consequently, I'm in the passenger seat, while she whips around curves like we're racing an invisible force.

"Are you trying to kill me or just scare me to death?"

Emeryn laughs. "Neither. Sorry. I'll slow down. Driving fast is something my dad and I used to do together."

"What happened to him?"

She scoffs. "Car wreck."

Thankfully, she turns into their driveway, and I release the air I was holding. I can't die if she were to wreck, but she can. "Are you sure this is the right address?" she asks, putting the car in park.

"Yeah. What did you expect?"

"I don't know. Something a little fancier?"

Jasper is waiting on the porch and is at my door in an instant. His brother is noticeably absent. Jasper opens the door and holds his hand toward me. "Welcome, ladies. You both look lovely today."

"Thank you." I smile.

"Where's Jackson?" Emeryn asks as she climbs out of the Porsche.

Jasper looks down before answering. "He had to leave."

Emeryn stops her movements. "Seriously? He left? Why?"

"I'm sorry, Emeryn. He left a few minutes ago with our cousin. I tried to make him stay."

"Celeste?" Tears fill her eyes.

"Go. I'll get back on my own."

"Are you sure?" She wipes a tear.

"Positive, and I understand." She jumps back in her car and slams the door. "Be careful!" I yell through a closed window.

"What the hell is wrong with him?" I ask as she flies out of the driveway.

"I wish I knew. Thank goodness our cousin was here, or I would have had to babysit. Ready to meet everyone?"

"When you say everyone, exactly how many is that?"

Jasper laughs, wrapping his fingers through mine, and leads me onto the epitome of a southern porch. Rocking chairs line the wall, complete with matching cushions and pillows.

"Are they here?" a woman calls from the kitchen the moment we enter the house.

A younger boy who could be Jackson's twin stands from the couch and runs in front of me. "Is this one yours or Jackson's?"

"Alex, this is Celeste, and she doesn't belong to anyone."

The boy looks me up and down, assessing everything about me. "What's wrong with your face? It's spotted."

"Those are my freckles."

"Why do you smell funny?" He sniffs the air in front of me.

"Alex, I think that's enough questions," Jasper reprimands his little brother. I sense Jasper's father before meeting him. His energy fills the house and is stronger behind the home.

"Your father is outside?"

"He is. Would you like to meet him?"

"Yes?" Honestly, I don't know whether I do or not.

Jasper leads me through a dining room already set for a meal and out a sliding glass door to the backyard. A large man with hair the same color as Jasper's is hitting golf balls from a homemade tee. The moment we exit the door, he turns, lifting his nose in the air.

"He smells me," I whisper.

"Yeah, I didn't tell him."

Jasper pulls me toward the Alpha lycanthrope, holding one hand in front of him. "Dad, don't jump to conclusions."

His father drops his golf club and transforms into the predator he is. "Why is she here?" he growls.

"Dad, this is Celeste."

"She's a vampire."

"I know." Jasper keeps his voice calm. "She's the one I've been seeing."

"Hello." I reach my hand forward, hoping he'll shake it. "Celeste Luquire."

"Luquire? As in Viktor Luquire?"

"You knew my father?" The large man reaches forward, shaking my hand.

"I did. He was mildly tolerable."

I smile. "My feelings precisely."

"You smell like him."

"Dad, that's weird," Jasper whispers.

Still holding my hand, his father introduces himself. "Xavier Daniels. It's a pleasure to meet you. My friends call me Xa." I take a minute to look at his features. He and Jasper share the same eye color and shape. While Jasper's features are narrower and more refined, his father's are large and bulky. He's definitely the Alpha.

"I've never had a vampire in my home before."

"I've never been in a lycan home before. We're even."

Xavier laughs. "I like her."

"Me, too," Jasper agrees, making the butterflies take flight once more.

"Come inside. My wife will have made enough to feed the entire pack."

Jasper grabs my hand, pulling me along behind his father. We enter the house and head into the kitchen. A heavyset woman is standing behind the stove, stirring a pot of something. "Mom?"

She turns around and takes a step back. "A vampire?"

"She's here with our son, and I knew her maker," Xavier fills in the blanks. Viktor wasn't my maker, but we don't have enough time to re-hash that saga.

"I haven't seen a vampire in ages." She wipes her hands on a wet apron. "I'm Leann. It's a pleasure to meet you." I shake her hand and smile.

"Thank you for the invitation." Leann turns around to the mounds of food she's prepared.

"Lunch will be ready soon. Did the other girl come?"

"No, ma'am. When she found out Jackson wasn't here, she went back to the dorm."

Leann and Xavier share a look. "Why don't we take a walk until it's time to eat?" Jasper asks, breaking the awkward glances of his parents.

"I'd like that."

I follow him out the same door we just came in, past the golf tee, toward what looks like a private pond. We sit on the edge of a small dock, hanging our feet over the side. "Your parents are nice."

Jasper laughs. "They're on their best behavior at the moment. Most of the time, they are nice, but my father is the Alpha, and he never lets us forget that."

"Why did Jackson leave?"

He throws a rock into the water, making a loud bloop. "Because he's an ass."

"What if he's not fit to be Alpha? I'm sorry. That was horrible of me to ask." I immediately regret putting him in the predicament of having to answer that question.

"You're not saying something that I haven't thought about many times. He's grown up a lot in the past few years, but you're right. He's not fit to be Alpha."

"What happens in that case?"

"There are no written rules. The firstborn son is always Alpha. That position would be passed to me if something were to happen to him."

"Is that something you would want?"

He scoffs. "Truthfully, no. I've never wanted to be Alpha."

"Food's ready," someone shouts from the house.

Jasper helps me stand. "I'm going to apologize in advance."

"For what?"

"If you thought Alex's questions were over the top, that's nothing compared to what my sister's going to do."

I take a deep breath, "Okay, I'm ready," I say, following him into the house.

"See, I told you she smelled funny," Alex announces from across the room.

A beautiful blonde girl is standing in the dining room, behind a chair. She looks like a mixture of Jasper and Jackson with blonde hair. "You *do* smell weird."

"I'm a vampire."

"What?" Alex runs from the room.

"She's not going to eat anyone," Jasper calls after him.

"I'm not taking any chances," he yells back.

Leann laughs. "He'll show back up when he gets hungry. I'm sorry. We don't have any... anything you'd eat here."

"It's fine. I'm not hungry."

"Well, I hate that you have to watch us eat. We could eat later."

"No. That's not necessary. I'm used to sitting around people while they eat." I slide into the chair next to Jasper.

"You're dating my brother?"

"Celeste, this is Samantha...my sister." Jasper's tone makes me laugh.

"It's nice to meet you, Samantha."

"I asked you a question. Are you dating my brother?"

"Samantha," her father reprimands.

"What? Jasper brings home a vampire for Sunday dinner, and I'm the one who gets in trouble. Doesn't that seem a little fucked up?"

"That's enough, young lady. Celeste is a guest in our home, and you will treat her as such."

"She's a fucking vampire. Maybe I should offer her a pint of blood for dessert?"

"Maybe I should go?"

"No. You're a guest, and you're welcome. Samantha,

you will say nothing else," Xavier reprimands his daughter. She rolls her eyes but stays quiet.

"How did you know my father?" I ask Xavier, hoping to ease the tension.

"Throughout the years, I've been down to New Orleans quite a bit. Edon and I worked closely together on several cases. On a few of those trips, I met Viktor. He was a good man."

"You'll have to forgive Samantha and Alex. There aren't a lot of vampires in this area, and they don't know much about them," Leann apologizes.

I smile. "It's fine. I understand not having much information. Have you met the new Alpha of New Orleans?"

"Christopher? I have."

"Then you know his mate, Amelia?"

Xavier looks at me. "Not personally, but I've heard about her."

I smile, knowingly. The rest of dinner passes quickly, and Alex eventually joins the family again for the meal.

I help clean up the dishes while Samantha continues to glare at me. Our conversation is light, and the heavy energy covering the house lifts the longer I'm here.

"Where did you meet, Jasper?" his mother asks, adding another dish to the dishwasher.

"We met downtown," he answers quickly. "Speaking of downtown, would you like to go? We could revisit the place we met." I fight to control the smile.

"That sounds like a great idea. I'd love to go back to that..."

"Restaurant," Japers fills in.

"Yes, that restaurant."

"Okay, I get it. You don't want me to know where you met. I'll stop being nosey," Leann says, loading another dish.

"Thank you for lunch. It was a pleasure to meet you all."

"Glad *you* enjoyed it," the grumpy blonde says.

A few minutes later, we're inside Jasper's truck and heading into town. "I'm sorry about Samantha. She takes after Jackson," Jasper announces as we enter downtown.

"She's just passionate." I laugh.

Jasper drives us to the riverwalk, overlooking the same river I've lived around for hundreds of years. Somehow, here, with Jasper, it has a completely different feeling. He takes my hand, leading us to the water's edge, when I spot something familiar.

"Is that Emeryn's car?" I point at the green Porsche, parked against the curb.

come out, come out, wherever you are

"THERE AREN'T a lot of green Porsches in Natchez. This has to be her car," Jasper answers, looking through the windows.

"I thought she was heading back to the dorm." I try calling her without luck. "She's not answering." I slide my phone back into my pocket.

"I'm sure she's fine. Maybe she just wanted to blow off some steam. Jackson knows how to piss someone off. It's his superpower."

"Yeah, maybe. Something doesn't feel right, though. Where's Jackson?"

"You don't think they're together, do you?" Jasper tries calling his brother. "He's not answering either." He dials another number. "Dammit, Taylor's not answering."

"Who's Taylor?"

"The cousin who's supposed to be watching Jackson."

"What aren't you telling me, Jasper? You know more than you're saying."

He leans against the Porsche. "I don't know anything. It's something you said that got me thinking."

"I've said a lot of things. You're going to have to be more specific."

"The missing girls. I can't help but wonder if Jackson had something to do with it."

"You said he was harmless."

He sighs, moving away from the car. "I did and still do, but something you said got me thinking. You said Emeryn lost her memories from their first date and the fact that she was drugged at the bar the first time we met. Something is off, and I can't help but wonder if my brother is involved."

"Jasper. If you think Jackson had anything to do with this, you need to go to the police."

"I can't, Celeste. Jackson's my brother, and he's a lycanthrope. I can't just waltz into the police station and announce that a werewolf might have taken the missing girls."

I move toward him. "If your brother is involved, he wouldn't be doing it alone. Nothing personal, but he doesn't seem that smart."

"I agree." Jasper's voice sounds sad. He looks up at me. "You don't think I'm involved?"

"You tell me, Jasper."

"Celeste. I would never do something like that. You can't think…"

"I don't know what to think," I interrupt. "Your brother is a loose cannon, and you're his handler. You tell me what I should think."

"Dr. Fitzgerald," he answers.

"What about him?"

"We need to talk to him. He and my father need to meet. The only way to figure this out is by joining forces."

"I'll get him. You get your father." I don't wait for a response. I walk away from the crowd and move vampire speed back to the college campus. I'm standing in the middle of the traffic circle within a few minutes.

I'm sure Oliver is staying on campus, but I'm not sure where. I stand still, searching for the familiar energy and finding it immediately. He's in the basement of the main building. One minute later, I'm banging on a door that looks like it leads to a dungeon. "Oliver!"

"Celeste?" The door opens quickly. "Has something happened?"

"May I come in?"

He looks both ways down the hall, before stepping aside. "Have a seat." The room is similar to my room in the dorm, only larger. Cinderblock walls line the square room. In the back corner, an unmade bed takes up space. A couch, television, and kitchen table are closer to the door.

"This room is used for traveling professors." He sits on the sofa. "Please." He points to the other end. "To what do I owe the pleasure of this visit?"

"You mentioned that you thought a lycan could be involved with the disappearances. Why?"

He takes a deep breath. "One of the first girls to go missing was eventually found deceased. Her injuries were consistent with an animal attack."

"Where was she found?"

"Floating in the river." He looks down with his words.

"Why has this been kept quiet? The girls here at Ravenwood need to be warned. This is crazy."

"That's why I'm here."

"No offense, Oliver, but what can one vampire do to save an entire city? These women are in danger. Have you met with the Alpha?"

"No. I've kept my investigation quiet."

"This doesn't make sense. If six young women are missing and one dead, the city of Natchez needs to be on an all-out manhunt. This isn't something to sweep under the proverbial rug, Oliver." I stand, moving across the room.

"The girl that was found was a vampire. Her head was nearly removed from her body, and she had deep gashes covering what was left of her."

"A vampire? How is that possible?"

"We're not indestructible, Celeste. Whoever killed her knew what she was. She was a baby vampire, without the knowledge or strength…"

"To fight off a wolf," I complete the sentence. "What about the other girls?"

"Human," he answers, knowing what I mean.

"Did you know her?"

"Yes. Not well, but I knew of her. She didn't deserve to die like that."

"That's why you're here…why a vampire is involved in human issues."

He nods. "Now, tell me what happened to bring you to my door on a Sunday afternoon. I know it wasn't for a friendly visit."

"We found Emeryn's car. She and I went to meet Jackson and Jasper's family to eat with them. When we arrived, Jackson was gone. Emeryn was upset and left to come back to the dorm."

"She never returned?"

"Her car is sitting empty in downtown Natchez."

"You think the drunk wolf from last night has something to do with it?"

I slide forward on the couch cushion. "God, I don't know. He's a loose cannon. He's capable of anything."

"What does his brother think?"

"Me being here was his idea. We thought it might be good for you to meet his father, the Alpha."

"Jackson's father is Xavier Daniels?" Oliver smirks. "That throws a wrench in, doesn't it? Aye, we need to have a conversation." He stands and grabs a set of keys from a table next to the door. "I'll drive."

I send a quick text to Jasper.

On our way to your house.

This should be fun.

Fifteen minutes later, Oliver pulls in front of the quaint farmhouse. "This is where the Alpha lives?" He climbs out of his Jeep. "This looks like it was designed and decorated on HGTV."

"I have no idea what you're talking about."

Oliver laughs. "I've been bored lately. Television has become my friend."

Xavier steps onto the porch, followed by Jasper, before we move two feet from the Jeep. "Celeste. When I welcomed you into my home, I didn't realize I was opening up a shelter. What do you want, Oliver?" he asks, glaring at my companion.

"We need to talk," he answers. "It's about something that involves the lycan." Xavier walks off the porch, heading toward the benches that are surrounded by yellow flowers.

"We'll talk over here. You're not welcome in my home."

"I understand."

I follow Oliver to the bench and sit next to him, not sure where the hostility is coming from. Jasper sits next to his father.

"What's this about?" Xavier asks.

"Several months ago, one in our community came up missing."

"How does that involve the lycan?"

Oliver is calm and doesn't respond to the jabs being thrown by Xavier. "Her body was found floating in the Mississippi River. She was nearly beheaded, and her body was covered in large scratches, consistent with an animal attack."

"You think she was murdered by one of my own? By a lycan?" Xavier connects the dots.

"Since then, five other women have also come up missing. All human and none have been found."

"Oliver, this is North Mississippi. Lycan aren't the only animals that roam the night. Hell, there are bobcats, panthers, and boars. It could've been any number of things that killed that girl."

Oliver nods. "Aye, but none of those are capable of producing the clean cut that would've separated her head from her body. Especially someone with vampire strength."

Xavier sighs. "How can I help?" I feel my body relax at his words.

Oliver crosses his legs. "I think we can agree, no matter if the girls are human, vampire, or lycan, this needs to stop."

"Agreed."

"Dad. The girl Jackson's been seeing may be missing."

"What do you mean?"

"When she found out Jackson wasn't here, she left, heading back to the dorm. We found her car downtown," I answer.

"That could be anything. There are dozens of restaurants within walking distance of downtown."

"True, but Emeryn isn't a 'go to a restaurant on my own' type of person."

"Might I suggest we go look for her?" Oliver stands.

"We'll meet you there," Xavier suggests as he and Jasper head toward a newer model SUV.

Oliver and I load into his Jeep and head toward downtown with the lycan following close behind. "That went better than I expected," Oliver announces with a smirk.

"What's the story between you two?" I ask.

"There's not much of a story, just the natural selection of things. You know, wolves and vampires."

It doesn't take long to reach downtown, and we find a parking spot not far from Emeryn's car. Since first discovering it, I've called her phone at least thirty times. It continues going straight to voicemail.

Xavier and Jasper walk around the car, running their hands over the shiny paint. "This is a nice car for a college student. Are we sure she's not involved in something more than college?" the Alpha asks.

"Her family has money," I answer.

"Why don't we split up and look for her?" he suggests. Jasper goes with his father since Xavier has no idea what she looks like. Oliver and I split up, taking different sides of the main street. I enter several stores, asking clerks if they've seen anyone matching her description. Each venue has been a bust. The last store on the block is a small boutique that looks right up her alley. The only employee, a young lady, is on her phone behind the desk. She jumps when the bell above the door rings.

"Hey," she greets me. "Let me know if I can help you with anything."

"Actually, I'm looking for my friend. She's a few inches taller than me, with dark hair and brown eyes. Very pretty. Has she been in here today?"

She laughs. "You're only the fifth customer of the day. I told my granny it was a waste of money to open on Sunday. One of the girls who came in fits your description." She walks to a blouse hanging on the rack. "She tried this on before a guy showed up."

"Guy? What guy?"

"A hot guy came in. Ignored me and went straight to her."

"What did he look like?"

"Dark brown hair, bright eyes, strong jawline, and built." She smiles, reliving her memory.

"Did she leave with him?"

"Yeah. She was excited to see him at first. She hugged him and was giggly. Then they were whispering something back and forth, and she wasn't happy anymore."

"What happened after that?"

"They left. He was holding her arm when they walked outside."

"Why didn't you call the police?"

"The police? Other than her looking annoyed, I had no reason to call the police. Hell, my boyfriend makes me feel like that regularly."

"Thank you." I run out of the store, looking for a familiar face. Xavier and Jasper are the first I find.

"She was here. Jackson found her in that boutique, and they left together. According to the clerk, she was happy to see him, but when they left, not so much."

"The young man at the bistro remembers seeing her walking with a young man toward the river," Oliver joins our group.

"Shit," Xavier mumbles. "Jackson, what the hell are you doing?"

visitors from the big easy

THE FOUR OF us head toward the riverwalk, hoping to find Emeryn or Jackson or some sort of clue. "Wasn't Taylor with him?" Xavier asks.

"Yeah, they left together, but neither of them is answering their phones," Jasper tells his father.

"Dad!" a voice calls from across the street. We turn, seeing Jackson and a guy I don't recognize, moving toward us. "What are you doing here?"

"Looking for you. Where have you been?" Xavier asks.

The boys look at each other. "Taylor wanted to meet up with a girl he's been talking to. She works at the boutique over there." He points at the same boutique where I talked to the employee moments earlier. He's lying, and everyone knows it.

"Did you find her?" Jasper asks, already knowing the answer.

"I did," Taylor answers. "We're meeting up later."

"Where's Emeryn?" I ask.

Jackson looks at me like I'm a nuisance. "I wouldn't know. Maybe you should ask her roommate."

"We have reason to believe she came here to find you," Oliver interrupts.

"Aren't you that teacher from the party who kept stalking me?"

"Jackson," Xavier reprimands. "Have you seen the girl?"

"No, sir," he answers. "I have not."

"He's lying," I blurt out.

"Shut up, bitch. Jasper, get your piece of ass under control."

Jasper is on his brother in a blink of an eye. He slams Jackson to the ground and growls louder than he should in public. "That's enough, boys." Xavier picks both of them up by the collars, setting them on opposite sides of the sidewalk. Taylor walks away, laughing.

"I'm taking them home," Xavier announces. "It was nice meeting you, Celeste."

Oliver wraps his arm through mine, pulling me in the opposite direction from the drama that just ensued. "That's why I don't hang out with lycan. Most of them have the IQ of a turd."

"What the hell was that, Oliver?"

"That was testosterone, mixed with supernatural ability, and a splash of asshole thrown in."

"We're no closer to finding Emeryn than when this

started. I don't care how insane he acted. He knows something."

"I don't doubt that for a minute. But we're not going to be able to reason with them. I have a plan."

"Care to share this plan?" We stop at Emeryn's car.

"Xavier may be the Alpha of this area, and he seems willing to work with us, but he's not going to give up his son easily. Even Alphas have an Alpha."

"Christopher? That's your plan," I ask.

"More like, Amelia. She's scarier than Christopher could ever be."

I laugh. "I take credit for that."

"You want to call them, or should I?"

I pull my phone out and lean against the Porsche. Amelia answers on the first ring, and I fill her in on every detail, ending with the events that just occurred. *"We'll be there tonight."* She doesn't hesitate, and my spirit lifts at the thought of seeing her again.

"They're coming tonight," I announce, hanging up the phone.

"Good. That'll give us more time to search while we wait."

We spend the next three hours searching and re-searching every store, restaurant, and hole in the wall, finding nothing. "This is no use, Oliver," I announce as we make our way across the city square for the hundredth time. "She's simply not here."

"I think you're right." My phone rings, and Amelia's number flashes on the screen.

"Hello?"

"We're here. I'm going to send you the address of our location. How soon can you be here?"

I show the address to Oliver. "Five minutes. That's right up the street," he whispers after seeing the address.

"Five minutes," I repeat.

"Good. See you soon." She hangs up, and Oliver leads me to his Jeep. He's right. It takes less than five minutes before we turn onto a street full of homes that rival each other in age. He pulls into the driveway of a three-story house, complete with a turret on top.

"This is impressive." I slide out of the passenger seat. "I don't remember Dad ever owning a home in Natchez, especially one this impressive."

"I don't believe this belonged to Viktor. Amelia must have acquired this on her own, or possibly it's Christopher's."

The door opens before we get to the bottom of the stairs. Amelia runs out, wrapping her arms around me, and I let tears flow. I return the hug, realizing how short she actually is.

After what feels like an eternity, she pulls away. "My God. You look...beautiful."

"Thank you. So do you."

A tall lycanthrope moves to her side. He's nearly a foot and a half taller than her. "Hello, Celeste. I'm Topher. I've heard a lot about you." I reach my hand toward him, which he bypasses, and wraps a long arm around my back. "If it weren't for you, I never would've met Amelia. Thank you."

"You're welcome," I answer as he pats my back heavily.

"Ollie!" Amelia moves on to Oliver and gives him a warm hug. "I've missed you."

"You, too," he answers. "It's been too long since I've been to the Big Easy."

"Come, sit down." Amelia leads us out of the grand foyer into a sitting room that looks like it was decorated during the Victorian Era. "We need to talk." She's staring right at me.

"My roommate, Emeryn…"

"No. We need to talk about this," she interrupts, moving her hand up and down. "How? I saw…we all saw what happened that night. You were turned back into the child."

"I'll explain later. Right now, our priority is Emeryn and the other missing girls."

"Topher called a meeting with the Alpha for this evening. He'll be here in an hour. We have time."

I take a deep breath before explaining the same thing I did to Jasper the night of the Hoopla. When I'm done, they're all staring at me in silence.

"What?" I ask, shrugging. "I was tired of being a kid."

"You traded being an immortal child for an average lifespan?" Amelia asks. She moves beside me, wrapping her hand around mine.

I nod. "I want to make the most out of what time I have left."

"Viktor would be so proud of you." Her words bring tears immediately. "Hell, I'm so proud of you."

"You're a vampire that will die of old age?" Oliver asks.

"As long as I don't kill anyone. Those are the rules. A life for a life."

The doorbell rings, and Amelia wipes her eyes. "It's showtime," she whispers.

"I'll get the door," Topher announces. I stand back as the door opens to the Alpha of North Mississippi.

"Xavier. It's good to see you again," Topher welcomes the lycanthrope into the home. Jackson walks in behind him. "I believe you know my wife, Amelia."

"Of course. It's good to see you again, Amelia. This is my son, Jackson. Future Alpha of North Mississippi."

"Please, have a seat." Topher motions to an empty settee on the other side of the room.

Jackson hasn't taken his eyes off me since they entered. He's undoubtedly trying to figure out why I'm here. I fight the urge to give him a black eye before he even realizes I've moved.

"You've met Celeste and Oliver," Topher says, pointing at the two of us.

"We have," Xavier answers. "I assume this is about the missing girls?"

"Celeste filled my wife in on all the details of the issue earlier. What is your take on it?" Topher asks.

Xavier glances around the room. "To be honest, today is the first time I've heard about it. Oliver and Celeste were kind enough to share the details with me."

"Oliver and several of his acquaintances believe a lycanthrope could be involved," Topher continues.

"He mentioned that. I reminded him that there are plenty of animals in this area that could inflict the same damage."

My eyes dart to Jackson, who's sitting next to his father, wearing a smug look on his face. I'd be willing to bet he knows something.

Amelia senses my feelings and moves closer to the lycanthrope. "Do you know what I am?" she asks Jackson as she sits next to him.

Jackson smiles. "Really hot?" he answers.

"Jackson," Xavier reprimands.

Amelia smiles. "That can't be denied." She giggles like a schoolgirl. "I'm also the only known hybrid in the world."

Jackson turns toward his father, who looks nervous for the first time. "Hybrid what?" he asks.

Amelia stands. "Would you like to tell him, Celeste?"

"I'll let you do the honors," I answer. At this point, I don't care if Jackson knows what I am.

She continues. "You see, my young friend, I am the

perfect combination of vampire and lycanthrope, making me something from your nightmares."

"Shit. Really? You're a half-vampire and half-wolf? How cool is that?" He nudges Xavier's side.

"It's super cool!" she responds. "Don't you think it's super cool, honey?"

"Super cool," Topher answers.

"What's she doing here?" He nods toward me.

"Celeste? She's the one who made me this way."

Jackson looks confused. "What does that mean?"

"It means she's the one who turned me into a vampire." She follows her words with a passive-aggressive smile.

He looks at me. "You're a vampire?" I nod. "Does... does Jasper know?"

"He does," I answer. "Since the first night we met. Seems like a future Alpha would've been able to pick up on what I am, wouldn't you think, Amelia?"

"One would think so, yes." She moves even closer to Jackson. "Being the best of both worlds gives me the ability to tear you to shreds in a heartbeat."

"I've seen it," I add. "It's not pretty."

"That's enough," Xavier says, standing and pulling his son with him. "We came here tonight in good faith. I've already told Oliver that the lycan are more than willing to aid this investigation in any way we can. Threatening the future Alpha is not part of that plan."

"Threatening? I was just sharing my abilities. He

was curious." Amelia moves back to the other side of the room. "I do apologize if that seemed threatening."

I've never seen Amelia act like this, but I'm here for it. Her behavior reminds me of my father when he was playing the part of an ancient vampire instead of a loving father. "Where's Emeryn, Jackson?" I continue the assault.

"Is that what this is about? You think I know where your whore of a roommate is?"

"Careful, Jackson. Remember when I said Celeste was my maker?" Amelia warns from across the room.

"Her car has been parked downtown all day, and the last person to see her said you were by her side."

He scoffs. "I haven't seen Emeryn all day. Even if I had, I wouldn't have done anything to hurt her. She's the best thing that's ever happened to me."

"Didn't you just call her a whore?" Oliver chimes in.

"I meant it with love."

God, Jackson truly is a psycho.

"Xavier, I'm sure you won't object to a search party tonight. The six of us can cover a lot of ground. Emeryn needs to be found." Topher acts like the Alpha he is.

"Agreed," Xavier responds. "We're here to do anything we can."

"That should make you happy," Amelia says to Jackson. "Especially since Emeryn is the best thing that's happened to you."

He smirks. "It does."

Topher slides the curtain back. "It's dark. We'll meet you at her car in an hour."

Xavier and Jackson stand, heading toward the door. "We'll be there. Thank you."

"Yes, thank you," Jackson echoes. "I do hope we find her." His voice is monotone and flat, and I've never wanted to kill anyone more than in this moment.

Amelia, sensing my thoughts, moves between us. "We'll be there." Waiting until they're out of earshot, she turns toward our small group. "That asshole of a kid knows something."

a boat to nowhere

TEN MINUTES LATER, Amelia and I are on our way to Emeryn's car. If Jackson is involved, he's going to hide any evidence that she's missing. The guys are doing the same but coming from a different direction. We decided to leave human transportation at the house and walk.

"I've only met that kid for a few minutes, but I don't like him," Amelia says as we move.

"Pretty much everyone who's met him feels the same."

"What do you know?"

"Well, his brother and I have been hanging out."

Amelia puts her hand on my arm to stop me. "His brother? Is his brother anything like him?"

"No. He's nothing like him." I can't hide the smile on my face.

"Celeste Luquire. What are you not telling me? Do you like this lycanthrope?"

"Maybe? I don't know."

"You have a crush? That's so sweet." Why do I want to hide right now? "Has this brother given any insight into Jackson's character?"

"Yeah. Jackson has issues."

"That's obvious. What kind of issues?"

"Honestly, I'm not sure. Jasper, his brother, has to basically babysit Jackson daily. He has a history of violence, and honestly, I don't know much more."

"He's next in line for the Alpha of this area," she states the obvious.

"Yeah, that's why he has to have a babysitter. Isn't there some clause for a future Alpha that's not a good fit or something? He can't be the only one in history that's not capable of performing his future role."

"I don't know, but it's something we definitely need to research. First, we need to find your roommate."

We turn the corner downtown and find Emeryn's car in the same spot as earlier. "Part of me was hoping it would be gone."

"Tell me about Emeryn," Amelia says as we approach the car.

"Her father is dead, and her mother likes to spend money. She's smart, sarcastic, and starved for attention."

"What do you mean?" Amelia looks around the car for clues.

"Jackson was the first guy she met here. When he showed her any sort of attention, she didn't question his tactics."

"What tactics?"

I lean against the metal railing in front of her car. "The first night we met Jackson and Jasper, she was drugged."

"Drugged? Like roofied?"

I shrug. "I guess. She was out of it for an entire day. Jasper got us home safely. The more I've learned about Jackson, the more I'm convinced he was involved."

"Probably," she answers.

"Afterward, he went a month without messaging her, then out of the blue wanted to spend time with her. Emeryn jumped at the chance again, but it was weird."

"How so?"

"Jasper said Jackson was home by ten o'clock, but Emeryn wasn't home for hours and had memories of meeting Jackson's family...which she didn't."

"Okay, what does that mean?"

"I don't know." I subconsciously cross my arms in front of my chest. "Amelia, did I make a mistake coming here?"

Amelia steps toward me. "Celeste, you are the smartest person I've ever met. I don't doubt for one minute that you researched every detail of this school and town." She pauses. "I don't think you made a mistake. You spent three-quarters of a century living the life of a prisoner, eternally trapped in the body of a five-year-old child. Viktor was an amazing father. He made sure you were protected and hidden for that entire time. You were alive, but you never lived."

I laugh at the irony. "I'm a vampire. Technically, I didn't live."

"You know what I mean." She smiles. "Viktor kept you under lock and key for your entire life. Now that he's gone, you've taken your life into your own hands, and I couldn't be prouder. You are a smart, beautiful, amazing young woman who chose what she wanted for herself and had the balls to do it." I wipe the tears streaming down my cheeks.

"I've missed you, Amelia."

"I've missed you, too. Don't stay hidden from me again. I want to know everything that you're doing. I want to be a part of it."

I nod, wrapping my arms around her. We cry together for a while before I pull away. "I never realized how short you are."

She pats my butt. "You're not too big to spank."

We sense someone otherworldly at the same time. We both freeze in place, searching for the source. *"Hide,"* I send the words to Amelia's mind, hoping we still have a connection.

She smiles, telling me she heard me. We move behind a large oak tree a few yards away from the car. It doesn't take long for the source to show himself. Taylor. Jackson and Jasper's cousin walks to the car, sliding his fingers across the hood. *"That's Jackson's cousin."*

He unlocks the car, and it roars to life. "He's taking her car," I announce, moving from our hiding spot. "What the hell?"

"He wants us to think she left."

I step in front of the car, blocking his escape. The asshole smiles when he realizes who I am. Tires squeal as he floors it, heading straight toward me. I jump out of the way just as the car flies by.

"That fucker was going to hit you. I'll follow him. You meet up with Oliver and Topher and keep looking for Emeryn." Amelia takes off running, moving faster than human eyes can track.

I move toward Oliver's energy, finding him and Topher a few blocks over with Xavier and Jackson. All four of them are staring into the river below. "What are we doing?" I ask, moving next to Oliver.

"Admiring the water," Oliver answers. "We all just got here."

"Has anyone checked her car?" Jackson asks, knowing it's no longer in the same spot.

"Do you feel anything, Topher?" I ask, ignoring the other two lycan.

"Nothing unusual. I sense lycan energy throughout the area, but nothing more than normal. What about you?" he asks.

I shake my head. He doesn't ask where Amelia is, and I'm grateful. "I think we should stick together to look."

"Because you were so successful last time," Jackson

spews.

"That's enough, son. I don't think you realize how this looks. The girl you're seeing is missing. Get your head out of your ass and help find her." Xavier's clearly had enough of his son's shit.

"I think we need to check her car again. Maybe it's gone, and she's safely back in her room."

"Has she texted you to let you know that's what she did?" I ask the asshole in front of me.

"No, but we're not at that point in our relationship yet."

"It's not a bad idea," Oliver adds. "Maybe Christopher can pick up on her trace."

"I'm better in wolf form," Topher answers.

Jackson shifts from foot to foot. "You shouldn't do that in public. Right, Dad?"

"No, that's a great idea." Xavier looks around. "The streets are relatively empty. We can pretend he's our pet."

Amelia appears in front of me, seemingly out of nowhere. "Everything good?" I ask.

"Of course. You should give me a tour of the university while we're here." Her words are code, telling me that's where Taylor took the car while the rest of our search party is staring at Amelia like she's lost her mind. "What?" she asks, shrugging.

Topher walks behind a tree and returns as a beautiful black wolf. Amelia moves next to him, and I laugh at the irony of the size of her "dog." His shoulders are even with the top of her head. "Yeah, this is completely believable. No one will question that he's a normal dog." Sarcasm oozes from my words.

Topher sticks his nose high in the air and turns toward a small grouping of trees. "He's caught her scent," Amelia announces. The two of them disappear into the forest. Jackson looks nervous.

"*Where are you?*" I ask.

"*A few miles away. What's Jackson doing?*" she asks through my mind.

"*Looking nervous.*"

"*Good. Keep them occupied.*"

"Should we follow them?" Jackson asks.

"No. I think our time is better spent here, where she was last seen." I purposefully lead the group to the spot where her car was parked.

"Look. I was right. She's gone. I bet she's in bed already." Jackson laughs.

"Text her," his father demands.

"She's probably..."

"Text her now," he growls. Jackson follows directions, pulling his phone out slowly. He types for a few seconds and slides the phone back into his pocket.

"Done. I'm ready to go home."

Topher and Amelia show back up with a familiar wolf in tow. "Jasper?" Xavier asks. "What are you doing here?"

"He's looking for Emeryn," Amelia answers. "We found him not far from where Topher lost the trail."

I move closer to Jasper's side. "What are you doing, Jasper? Did you have something to do with Emeryn going missing?"

"No," Amelia answers. "He caught her scent and was searching, like us."

I'm not sure why Xavier seems upset, but anger covers his face.

"He says he was just trying to help," Amelia continues.

"Go home," Xavier demands. What the hell? Why is he angry with Jasper but allows Jackson to act like a giant ass?

"No." Topher walks from behind a tree, wearing a pair of torn shorts. "He stays. We need all the help we can get."

Jasper follows suit and walks out wearing a pair of shorts that are so short they threaten to climb into places they shouldn't. I can't hide the smile at his appearance. "Sorry, it's all I could carry." He tugs the legs of the shorts, trying to lengthen them.

"I lost her scent up the river a few miles. She wasn't alone," Topher says, looking around our small group. "She was with several lycan I didn't recognize."

"What are you saying?" Jackson asks.

"I'm saying, I don't recognize the scent of the lycan she was with. I felt like that was pretty plainly spoken. In human form, lycan smell different than wolf form." Topher is clearly as annoyed with Jackson as Xavier.

"Did you recognize the scent?" I ask Jasper. He shifts nervously.

"Jasper, answer the question," Xavier demands.

"It was Jackson."

"That makes sense. We were together earlier today," Jackson says with a smile.

Xavier turns, facing his son. "You said you hadn't seen her today."

"I must have misspoken," he answers.

Xavier shifts into wolf form without warning. In less than a second, he's on top of Jackson, pinning him to the ground. Saliva drips from the ends of his long teeth. "Dad, stop." Jasper jumps to his brother's aid. "This isn't helping."

The giant wolf backs away. I step in between the father and son, tired of playing games. I turn, facing Jackson, and stare into his eyes. "Celeste?" Amelia questions. "Are you alright?"

"Where is she, Jackson?"

"Shut up, bitch."

For the first time in a year, I bare my teeth, turning into the monster I've worked hard to suppress. I fly toward him, pinning him to the ground before he's noticed I moved. "I'll ask you one more time. Where. Is. Emeryn?"

Jackson's eyes dilate as he falls under my spell. "With the others. I don't know what happens to them after the boat picks them up."

"What boat?" I continue.

"The boat from Louisiana," he answers.

"What are you saying?" Jasper whispers from behind me. "Did you have something to do with the other missing girls? Did you hurt them?"

"I never hurt them. I just give them to people who will." His eyes regain their normal look, and a smirk covers his face. "Get off me, bitch."

I stand, and Amelia moves between the two of us, pushing me back. She no doubt senses the anger boiling deep inside. *"He's not worth it."*

"I need to correct that," Jackson adds. "I never harm the human ones. That vampire girl wasn't their type. I had to take care of it."

"Jackson. What have you done?" Xavier roars.

"Chill, Dad. I owed some bad people a lot of money. This was the easiest way to pay that back." He smiles as he speaks. The bastard doesn't feel any empathy for the women he's sent into hell or the one he murdered.

"You sold five women into who knows what as payment for a debt and killed another?" Jasper repeats his brother's words. "Are you an idiot?"

"Jas, you know me, man. I do what I need to do."

I move closer to Jackson. "You are a son of a bitch."

He laughs. "Well, my mother is a lycanthrope."

Xavier reacts before I can. He's on top of his son in the blink of an eye, pushing him against a nearby tree and pulling his hands behind his back, forcing a scream. "Where are they?" he spews.

The smirk disappears from his face, and his

eyebrows bend in exasperation. "I don't know. I told you. My job is to get them to the boat."

"Enough," Topher moves closer. Xavier steps away from his son, responding to his Alpha. Topher moves inches in front of Jackson and towers over the younger wolf. "Contact these people and tell them we want to meet."

"That's not how it works. They contact me. I don't contact them."

"How often?" I ask.

"Whenever they feel like it." His shoulders raise slightly, and the smirk returns.

Topher moves closer yet. "Maybe I didn't make myself clear. You will contact the people in the boat, and you will tell them we want to meet."

"Or else?" Jackson asks.

"Are you prepared to find out?" Amelia's voice is full of venom.

"I'll let you know when I make contact." Jackson loses a bit of his arrogance.

"You have two hours," Topher announces.

"I'm sorry." Jasper apologizes as Jackson and Xavier walk away. "I had no idea."

"Why do you have to babysit him?" Amelia interrupts. "You had to have some kind of idea."

"He doesn't think the same way as most people. He doesn't understand how circumstances work or his role in them. He's been like that since I can remember. But this...I would never have thought Jackson was capable of doing something like this."

"He has no place as Alpha," Topher joins our conversation. "Alphas hold the responsibility of keeping their pack safe. Your brother is not fit for that role."

Jasper kicks the broken concrete shards in front of him. "It's why our father worked so hard to help him."

"Yeah, looks like it's working." Amelia crosses her arms in front of her chest. "Emeryn could be anywhere at this point."

"We'll find her." Oliver moves to my side. "The others, too."

bobby and jimmy

TWO HOURS PASS in a slow daze. Nothing has been accomplished while we wait for Jackson to make contact with the...I don't even know what to call them. Kidnappers, traffickers, bad guys? Assholes. That works. Topher has spent most of the time with Jasper, asking questions about his brother, while Amelia, Oliver, and I search the area for any clues we may have missed earlier.

"Are you sure that kid isn't involved in this mess?" Amelia nods toward Jasper.

I stare at the dark-haired lycanthrope. "A few days ago, I would have said yes. Now, I'm not sure. He loves his brother and has spent his entire life protecting him."

"That's not fair to him. What kind of life is that? He's a prisoner, controlled by his brother's instability."

"That sounds slightly familiar," I add.

Amelia sets the large rock she moved back in place. "Oh, Celeste. I'm sorry. That was selfish of me to say. I didn't mean it like that."

"I know. Maybe that's why we were drawn to each other. We're both prisoners of our lives."

"Topher thinks Jasper should be the next Alpha."

I stop moving. "Can that happen? I thought the next Alpha was something that was predestined or something. It's clear Jackson isn't fit for the job, but can they just skip him?"

Amelia looks down. "Only if Jackson dies."

"What are you saying?"

She continues moving the large rocks that line the riverbed. "I'm not suggesting anything. I'm simply stating facts." She doesn't need to finish her thought for me to know what she's saying. Jackson can't become Alpha. Whatever happens to keep that from occurring happens.

Jasper and Topher join us on the riverbank. "They're on their way back," Jasper announces as he gracefully leaps from rock to rock.

"Any luck with the contact?" Oliver asks. Lights flash on from the other side of the river, as a boat roars to life and begins to work its way toward us.

"There's your answer," Amelia mumbles as the engine moves closer.

"That could be anyone. There are plenty of boats on this river." I move toward the water's edge.

"That's them," Jackson says from the rocks above. "They're not real nice."

"Neither are we," Amelia answers. The three of us join the awaiting lycan at the top of the rocks and wait for the boat to dock.

It doesn't take long for two men to exit and move up the dock in our direction. Jackson pushes past me, knocking into my shoulder as he walks down the metal ramp toward them.

"What the hell is this about?" one of the men whispers. He's wearing a pair of custom-tailored khaki pants and a pink button-down designer shirt.

"They want to join in," Jackson whispers back.

The man looks around Jackson at the group staring down at him. "Why?"

"Why what?"

"Why do they want in?" His eyes land on me as he speaks.

"They want a cut."

The man scoffs. "Fuck off, boy." He moves to turn.

"I think you might want to talk to us," Oliver calls toward the men.

"And why would I want to do that?"

"Because we're rich," Amelia answers.

"If you have money, why the hell do you want in on this?"

"You can never have enough," Oliver answers.

The man turns back toward our group, and again his eyes fall on me. "Who is she?"

Jackson turns toward me. "She's nothing more than a fucking bitch." Hate spews from his lips.

"I want her," the man says. The words roll off his tongue in sticky sweetness.

"She's not for sale," Topher announces.

"Then we don't have a deal." He turns, heading back to the boat.

"Wait!" I call after him. He stops walking.

"Celeste, what are you doing?" Amelia's voice sounds through my mind.

"If I go, can you assure me of my safety?" I try to sound as innocent as a naive eighteen-year-old girl would be.

He scoffs, making my stomach curl. "Of course, darlin'. I wouldn't dream of hurting you."

"No," Jasper says, moving to my side. "You don't know what you're walking into."

"I have to do something," I whisper.

"Celeste? Are you sure about this?" Amelia asks.

"No," I answer truthfully. *"Right now, I'm all Emeryn has. I have to try. I'm stronger than they are. They can't hurt me."*

"You don't know that," she retorts. *"The last vampire girl showed up dead."*

"That was because she was young. I'll be fine."

"What if...what if you have to kill one of them?"

I don't answer. Instead, I move toward the boat without looking back. Passing by Jackson, I slam my shoulder into his, knocking him close to the edge.

"You're going to be fun," the creepy man says with a smile. "The spicy ones are always more fun."

"Spicy, my ass," Amelia echoes. *"We're going to follow you. Stay in contact with me at all times. If you don't answer me for three minutes at any point, I'm coming in and killing everyone without a second thought. Do you understand?"*

"Now who's acting like the mom?"

"Celeste. I'm not kidding."

"I know, and I love you for it."

"You're even prettier up close. You'll fetch a lot of money with that hair." The man grabs a long curl, wrapping it around his fingers.

"If you take her, what's in it for us?" Oliver says from behind.

"Someone will be in touch," the man answers.

"That's not how this is going to work," Topher interrupts. "You take her, we take one of yours. That's the rule. Take it, or leave it."

"Bubba, get out here," the man yells to someone inside the boat. Another man climbs from underneath the hull and jumps onto the dock. It's not until he's moved into the lights that I realize he's just a kid. Maybe thirteen or fourteen at the oldest. My new captor slaps Bubba on the back of the head as he passes by. "You be a good boy and do whatever he wants you to do for him." My stomach flips thinking about the implications of his words.

Bubba moves in front of Oliver. He barely comes to Oliver's chin. He's nothing more than skin and bones.

"How's that?" my captive yells. "He's a good boy and follows orders...don't ya, Bubba?"

"Yes, sir," he answers.

"Someone will be in touch with you. If you can provide us more like this one," he runs his hands through my hair again, and I resist the urge to kill him on the spot, "then we can continue this little project."

"We can," Topher answers, taking on the role of leader.

"Good. You'll get a call tomorrow." The man jerks my arm, pulling me toward the boat.

"Don't kill him," Amelia warns.

"Get in," the man throws me into the same area Bubba emerged from. The boat is small and smells like shit.

"Where are we going?"

"Louisiana," he answers. "No more questions. Sit down, and shut up before I make you." I don't fight. I sit on a narrow ledge that lines the outside of the hull. "You sure are pretty. I may take a turn with you before we send you down the river."

A taller man brings the boat to life, and we move away from the dock in Natchez, heading who knows where. "You can't do that," he reprimands. "They're not for us."

"Shut up. They'll never know if I take a turn with this one." He turns toward me. "You wouldn't tell our little secret, would you?" He moves closer to me. "Hell, you're not like the rest of them. I can tell you'd like it."

It's getting harder by the minute to keep from killing this asshole. Fuck the rules. The boat docks on the other side of the river, and my new friend wraps his arm around mine, pulling me toward the dock. I feel Amelia, Oliver, and the lycan nearby. I don't know where they are, but they're not far.

"Amelia?"

"I'm here," she answers. *"We're all here. If you change your mind about this stupid idea, tell me. We'll be on them before they know what's happening."*

"I have to find her," I answer.

"Let's go," my captive says, pulling me up the dock, past the large rocks. Where we got off is nothing more than a boat launch. While the tall man loads the boat onto a trailer, my friend forces me into the back of a bright red truck.

"Hard to lay low in this thing." I laugh.

"Who says we're trying to lay low? Don't do anything dumb. I'll be back." He slams the door, locking me inside the vehicle. I could be out in a heartbeat, but I'm determined to find Emeryn. The only way to do that is by going through what she went through.

A few minutes later, the trailer is hitched, and we're heading down a deserted highway. "Where are we going?"

"Shut up," the tall man who's driving answers.

"We're taking you to meet some friends," the other answers.

"You should've put a blindfold on her," the driver says.

"What the hell does it matter, Jimmy? It's not like she's ever been here before." He turns toward me. "Have you?"

"Louisiana? No, I've never been out of Mississippi before."

These two idiots aren't in charge of whatever this is. They're nothing more than errand boys, just like Jackson.

I've lost track of how far we've traveled when we finally stop. The bright headlights of the truck bounce off the blacked-out windows of a wooden shack in front of us. After miles of pine trees, everything looks the same.

"Where are we?" I ask.

"That's not your concern," Jimmy answers. He's obviously the smarter of the two. "Take her inside. I'll wait out here." He opens a box on the floorboard. "Put these on her." He throws a pair of handcuffs at my no-name friend.

"She's not going to run, are you, sweetheart?"

"No," I answer.

"Put them on her anyway," he demands. I hold my wrists in front of me, making it easier for him.

"We've stopped at a wooden house that looks like it's about to fall down. Nothing around us except tall pine trees."

"We're with you," Amelia confirms. I feel them nearby, which gives me strength.

The back door opens, and my new friend pulls me out of the truck. "Come on, Red. You can answer the age-old question about the curtain matching the drapes." I have no idea what he's talking about, and the tone of his voice tells me I don't want to know.

"There's no time for that, Bobby." Bobby. That's his name.

"Bobby and Jimmy. Their names are Bobby and Jimmy."

"Got it," Amelia answers.

Jimmy gets out, following behind us as we go inside the worn-out shack. The door opens and leads to a second door that looks much newer than the first. He knocks three times and steps back as the door opens. A dark-skinned man steps out, holding a gun in front of him.

"The fuck do you two want?" His accent is thick with Louisiana Cajun.

"We have another one."

"It ain't time for another one. You two are stupid." He waves the weapon in Jimmy's face.

"This one sort of fell in our laps. We need to talk to Bandit."

The gunman shifts back and forth. "Bandit isn't taking visitors right now."

"Then we'll take this one and go," Jimmy answers.

"Wait." The gunman moves closer, lifting my curls

into his hand and letting them fall gracefully to my side. "How much?"

"Twenty thousand," Jimmy answers.

"Twenty thousand? You really are an idiot."

"Then let me talk to Bandit."

The door opens wide, and another man comes outside. "Take her to the holding cell while I take these two to see Bandit."

Out of nowhere, a blindfold is wrapped around my eyes, and I'm pulled away from my buddy, Bobby. My shoes click across the floor, and I recognize the sound of marble tile as we move. Smells of body odor, different kinds of foods, and one that I recognize in an instant fill my nose. Emeryn's been here. I'm pulled to a stop as someone beside me rattles keys around and unlocks a heavy metal door. I'm shoved inside, landing on the floor. The handcuffs are taken off, and the door slams behind me. I sit up quickly, pulling the mask from my eyes.

"Celeste?" a familiar voice whispers from the corner of the room. "Oh, my God. Celeste, is that you?" Emeryn runs in front of me, wrapping her arms around my waist.

back to the big easy

EMERYN PULLS AWAY, wiping tears from her cheeks. "How are you here? Did he bring you here, too?"

"I can't explain everything right now." I step back, assessing her from head to toe. "Are you alright?"

"Physically, yes. Mentally, no. Jackson sold me to those bastards."

"I'm sorry, Emeryn. I'm here to help you."

"How the hell are you going to help? We're locked in the same damn room."

I glance around the dark room and spot two cameras pointing down at us. I don't want whoever is watching us to know anything. "Jackson sold me, too."

"How could I be so stupid, Celeste? I fell for his lies. Hook, line, and sinker."

"You're not stupid. You just have really poor taste in men."

She laughs, wiping more tears. Her black eyeliner is

smeared across her cheeks, and one eyebrow is nearly rubbed off. She wraps her arm through mine. "I'm so sorry I got you into this."

"Don't be. I found you. That's all that matters."

"Who's going to find you?" she asks. I feel the lycan and vampire energy surrounding the shack.

"Amelia?"

"We're here," she answers.

"Emeryn is here."

"Oh, thank God. I feel like we have two options. One—we storm the building and leave no one alive. Two—we wait it out and go for the people in charge."

I turn toward my roommate. "We're going to be okay."

"How can you be so sure, Celeste?"

I lead her to a wooden bench in the corner of the room. "Because I've been through worse."

"I like option one, but option two is the only way to keep this from happening to anyone else. They'll find someone else to do their dirty work for them once Jackson's out of the picture. We have to keep this from reoccurring." I don't hear anything from the other end. *"Amelia?"*

"I'm here. Topher's having to keep Jasper from following through with option one. Even though he has an asshole for a brother, he's growing on me."

I can't hide the smile that forms.

"How can you smile at a time like this?" Emeryn asks.

I wrap her hands in mine. "Because we're going to

get out of here, and we're going to take this entire shit-hole down with us."

"This is a horrible thing for me to say, but I'm glad you're here with me." She squeezes my fingers as she speaks.

"I'm glad I'm here, too. We're going to get out of this unscathed."

"I don't know why, but I believe you."

"Good. How often do they come into this room?"

Emeryn looks up. "They brought me dinner and then you. I haven't been here too long."

"Have you been alone since you got here?"

"Yes." Her voice sounds shaky again.

"*Celeste?*" Amelia calls through my mind.

"*I'm good.*"

"*We have a plan. Are you somewhere that the two of you will be safe until the sun comes up?*"

I look around the room. "*I think so. I'll make sure she's safe.*"

"*I know you will. Sit tight for a few hours, and trust me.*"

"Emeryn, why don't you get some sleep? I'll stand guard."

She laughs. "What do you think you'd be able to do, Celeste? You weigh a hundred pounds soaking wet. Those are grown-ass men."

"I can handle myself. Get some rest."

She curls on the bench next to me, resting her head

on my thigh, never letting go of my hand. "Wake me when you want to sleep."

"Okay." Her breathing slows down within minutes, and her hand goes limp. I stare into every corner of the room, memorizing each shadow and each flaw in the sheetrock. Even with supernatural hearing, I don't pick up on any conversations or movements from outside this room. If I didn't know better, I'd swear the building was empty. Without a window or my cell phone, I've lost track of time and have no idea if it's daylight yet.

Amelia has been quiet since we spoke earlier. In the silence, my mind plays over all the craziness and good that college has brought. I replay mine and Jasper's kiss, bringing tingles to every part of my body.

Minutes, hours, days...I have no clue which...later the door opens, flooding the room with light. "There you are." Bobby saunters in, moving in front of me. Emeryn jumps up, and her heart rate speeds up as soon as she sees him. Bobby grabs a handful of my hair, massaging his fingers through the ends. "Your hair reminds me of fire. How about you and I go make some fire of our own?"

"I'm not interested," I retort.

"I didn't ask if you were interested." His fingers grip tighter, pulling my head to the side.

"Stop!" Emeryn yells. "Leave her alone."

"Shut up, bitch." Bobby backhands Emeryn on the cheek, slamming her head into the wall behind her.

I grab the hand clenched in my hair. Forcing his

fingers backward until they touch the top of his hand. Bobby looks at me with complete confusion as his face contorts into a silent scream.

"You owe her an apology." My words are soft as I continue my assault.

"I'm... I'm..." he struggles for the words.

"You're getting close. Keep trying." I refuse to release my grip.

Tears fill Bobby's eyes as his middle finger breaks at the joint, forcing his bone to protrude through the skin. "I'm sorry!" he shouts.

I instantly release his hand as the smell of blood fills the room. Bobby runs through the door, leaving it cracked behind him.

"Celeste? How did you do that?" Emeryn sounds confused.

"I told you I can take care of myself. Someone else will be here in a moment. Let me do the talking." Emeryn doesn't question me and slides backward on the bench.

Just as I suspected, Jimmy is next in the room. "What happened in here?" He eyes the blood staining the concrete floor in front of me.

I don't answer.

Jimmy moves in front of me. "I said, what happened in here?"

I slowly lift my eyes, making eye contact with him. "He fell. Landed on his finger, and it broke. Poor guy."

Jimmy has enough discernment to see the

monster I keep hidden through my facade. He backs away slowly, keeping his eyes on mine. "What are you?"

"I'm a college freshman who's been looking for her missing roommate."

He backs out of the door, closing and locking it behind him.

"Celeste? What's going on in there?"

"Nothing major. Just broke an asshole's finger. Other than that, nothing. What about out there?"

"Whatever you did has them in a tizzy. The men from the boat are leaving. One of them has his hand wrapped in towels and is leaving a B-positive blood trail."

"What is Jackson doing?" I ask.

"Xavier took him back to the city. He needed to get out of here. He was losing his shit."

"I believe that was already lost. What about Jasper?"

"He won't leave Topher's side. There's a lot of movement going on outside. It looks like they're about to move you. You still want to go through with this?"

"Yes," I answer without hesitation.

Just as Amelia warned, the door creaks open. Three men wearing masks enter, grabbing both of us, and dragging us to the door. I resist my natural instinct to fight. Instead, I pretend to be terrified. Blindfolds are slipped over my eyes, and my hands are pulled tightly behind me. No one speaks as they push us over the marble tile and outside the doors. Once outside, what sounds like a rolling door slides up right before we're thrown into the back of what I'm assuming is a truck of some sort.

"Celeste?" Emeryn whispers.

"I'm here." I slide backward until my back hits a wall.

"Where are they taking us?"

"I'm guessing to a larger city. Most likely New Orleans."

"New Orleans? Why?"

"Because it's easier to hide us in a big city." I break the zip ties holding my hands and lift the blindfold. Just as I suspected, we're in the back of a box truck, surrounded by moving boxes. I reach over, pulling Emeryn's blindfold up.

"How'd you get loose?" she asks.

I smile without answering. "Emeryn, I'm not going to let anything happen to you, but I need you to trust me."

She nods. "I trust you."

"We're safe. I know it may not feel like that at the moment, but we are. There are people following us who will make sure nothing happens to us. We're not the first women who have fallen victim to these creeps. Five other women are missing, and one has been killed." Tears fill Emeryn's eyes. I put my hand on top of hers. "We have a chance to stop this from happening to anyone else. Are you willing to do that?"

"Yes." Her voice is weak.

"If at any time you change your mind, all you have

to do is tell me, and I'll get you out of here. Do you understand?"

"Yes," she whispers.

"When the truck slows down, I'm going to pull your blindfold back over your eyes." She nods.

"Amelia? Are you there?" I ask through our connection.

"We're here. Hanging back from the truck. You guys, okay?"

"We're good. Can you tell which direction we're going?"

"South. Oliver thinks they're taking you to New Orleans."

I laugh. *"That's what I thought. Just a little bit of irony there."*

"I know, right?"

"Celeste? Can I ask you something?" Emeryn asks, interrupting my silent conversation.

"Of course."

"Are you a...a vampire?

"What? Like the creatures in books and movies?" I laugh at her statement.

"Yes. No. I don't know. If vampires are real, I'm sure they're not like the ones in books. It's just that I've seen you do things that only a vampire can do."

I lean my head against the side of the truck. "Like what?"

"The first night you were there, I know you were drinking blood, and...and you don't sleep. I've seen you at night. You pretend to sleep." She takes a deep breath. "You broke that man's hand like it was nothing. That's not normal, Celeste."

"I told you I can take care of myself."

"I can take care of myself, but I can't bend a grown man's hand backward and break his fingers without even trying."

Should I tell my darkest secret?

"The friends that are following us...are they vampires too?" she interrupts my thoughts.

I stare at my roommate not sure how to respond. "You're not scared?"

"Of you? No. The humans that put us in the back of this truck are far scarier than you. Besides, if you were going to eat me, you'd have done it by now." She pauses. "That woman that brought you the first day. Was she the one who created you? Was she your mother?"

"No, my mother is dead. I killed her." Emeryn looks up quickly, rethinking her earlier statement. "My mother was an evil, horrible woman. The woman who brought me was my nanny, my caregiver."

Emeryn nods. "I trust you and your friends. Thank you for coming after me. I thought I was going to die without anyone ever knowing where I went." She grabs my hand and squeezes. "If you're hungry, you can take some of my blood."

I laugh. "I don't drink human blood. Thank you for

the offer, though." The truck begins to slow, and I slide both of our blindfolds back into place. Seconds after we stop, the door of the truck slides open, and a bucket is thrown inside.

"Go pee," a deep voice demands.

"I don't need to go," I retort.

"Try."

"How do you expect us to go to the bathroom with our hands behind our backs and blindfolds covering our eyes."

A deep sigh comes from behind us. "Shit." I hear the sound of someone jumping into the truck with us. "Try anything, and I'll shoot you on the spot. Understand?"

"Seems like a huge profit loss if you shoot one of us."

"I'm willing to risk it. Get up," he demands to Emeryn, cutting the zip tie on her wrists. I slide the blindfold up enough to see what's going on. He stands over her as she squats over the bucket, letting a few dribbles hit the bottom.

"Happy?" she asks.

"Very." He slides a new zip tie on her wrists and moves toward me. "Get up."

"I'm good. I don't need to go."

"Suit yourself." He moves back toward the door, leaving the bucket with us. As he moves to slide the back of the truck closed, a familiar face pops up behind him.

"Hello," Jasper says with a smile. "I believe you have cargo in the truck that I'm highly interested in."

"Fuck off, boy," bucket man spews.

"You see, I can't do that." In an instant, Jasper shifts into wolf form, slicing the man in half.

"Celeste? What was that?" Emeryn asks, not being able to see through her mask.

"That was our rescue crew," I answer as a giant wolf jumps inside the truck.

"Is that...a wolf?" Emeryn asks the moment I rip the blindfold from her face. "Celeste! Move!" Emeryn shouts, worried for my safety.

I pull the dismembered body completely into the back of the truck and quickly close the sliding door. "How is this sticking with the plan?" I ask as Jasper shifts back into human form. "I thought we were going with..." My words fail me when I realize Jasper is standing in front of me naked. Pink covers his cheeks as he covers the front of him. I turn, giving him privacy. In the years I've been on this earth, this is the first time I've ever seen a man naked other than photographs and paintings.

"I saw a chance and took it," he answers. "I wasn't going to watch this shit show any longer."

A box in the back corner of the truck is torn open with several new-looking garments hanging from it. The truck lunges forward as I grab a pair of blue flowered shorts and a matching shirt, still attached to the hanger. "Here, put this on." I throw the clothes behind me.

"I'm good," he offers a few moments later.

"What the fuck, Jasper? Are you...I don't even know how to ask what I'm asking. Are you a *werewolf?*" Emeryn is on her feet. A look of horror covers her face.

Jasper pulls the shirt over his head, making him look like an elderly tourist. "We prefer the term lycan."

She turns to me. "Did you know this?"

I sigh before answering. "Yes."

"Jackson?"

"He's one, too."

Emeryn collapses on top of an unopened box. "Holy shit. I was sold by a werewolf."

"For what it's worth, I'm sorry. We're not all like him." Jasper sits on a box a few feet away. "Jackson's had issues his entire life, but nothing like this. I should've stopped him. I'm sorry I let it get this far."

"For the first time in my life, I'm speechless," Emeryn says, staring at the two of us.

"Topher and Amelia are in the front of the truck." He turns to me. "When I took out that guy," he nods toward the body, "they took control of the driver. There's only one man left, and he's being kept alive."

"Why?" Emeryn whispers.

"We have to put a stop to this. He's our only chance. We need to find out who's in charge."

"The men back at the shack, they talked about

someone named Bandit," I answer. "I had the feeling that whoever the Bandit is, they're in charge."

"What are we going to do now?" Emeryn's voice has lost its fight.

"We're going to end this, once and for all," Jasper answers.

the bandit

BEING LOCKED in the back of the truck, I've lost track of time. Emeryn and Jasper have both fallen asleep, giving me time to consider every possible outcome of this madness. Amelia hasn't said much other than to assure me that everything was under control and that she and Topher were both in the front with the lone idiot from the club.

The truck starts and stops several times as we roll through what feels like a town. *"Are we in New Orleans?"*

"Home, sweet home," Amelia answers. *"The driver is taking us to their drop-off point. I'm pretty sure we're heading toward the docks."*

"How do you know he's not taking us somewhere to kill us?"

"I might have used a little compulsion on him," she answers. The fact that Amelia's become a powerful

vampire without my help makes me both sad and proud.

A few more starts and stops until the truck comes to what feels like a permanent stop. *"We're here. You need to slide the blindfold back in place and act like your arms are bound. In order to stop this, you need some good acting chops. We'll be close."*

"I understand," I answer. "We're here. Emeryn, put your blindfold back on. Jasper, hide."

Jasper doesn't question me. He slips between two larger boxes toward the front of the truck, moving the body of the dead man with him. Emeryn slides her blindfold over her eyes and takes a deep breath. "What's about to happen?" she whispers.

"I don't know. We need to act terrified."

"That's not a huge stretch." She laughs.

The back of the truck slides open, and someone steps inside. "Get up," a deep voice demands. A hand grips my shoulder, shoving me forward. "Walk." I hear Emeryn whimper behind me and the sound of her shuffling feet.

"Where's the driver," someone says from behind the truck.

"He had to take a piss," the man shoving me answers. "These two are going to bring big bucks." A hand slides down my arm and across my butt. I fight the urge to break whoever the hand belongs to in half. Instead, I shudder at the touch, pretending to be the scared little girl they think I am. His laugh is deep and annoying. He enjoys the fear he thinks he brought. "Stop," he orders. "Turn around and step down back-ward." I follow directions, stepping onto the concrete below. Behind me, he gives Emeryn the same direc-tions. I feel her step beside me as the two of us stand side by side.

"These two are rather nice. Take them inside."

"I'd rather keep this one for myself. I'm partial to redheads." My hair is pulled, jerking my head to the side. "She reminds me of my niece." Disgusting asshole.

It takes everything I have not to kill both of them on the spot. *"Amelia, what's going on?"* I ask through our connection.

"You and Emeryn are on the docks."

"Emeryn's scared."

"Want me to call it?" she asks.

"Not yet."

Bony fingers wrap around my arm, and I'm half shoved, half pulled in the opposite direction of the water. Emeryn is still at my side, and I'm grateful I'm here for her. The sound of scraping metal echoes off nearby walls as the two of us are shoved through a door.

"Shit." Amelia's voice yells.

"What's happening?"

"Jasper is getting out of the truck."

"Dammit, Jasper. He needs to stay hidden." I hear the sound of wispy wind and a soft grunt behind me.

"Got him," Amelia says. *"He's not happy."*

"Tell him I'm okay."

"Already did. He's not convinced."

A hand pushes my shoulder, forcing me to sit. Emeryn is pushed down next to me. "What are you going to do with us?" Emeryn asks.

"Shut up," one of the men answers. The blindfold is ripped from my eyes, and I realize we're inside an empty warehouse.

"Where are we?" I ask.

"I said shut up, bitch." The man raises a hand, ready to backhand me. No matter how hard I try, I struggle playing the damsel in distress. I stare the man in the eyes, sending a silent warning. Instead of slapping me, he lowers his hand and clears his throat. "Put them in the dungeon. D will be here tomorrow." He turns, leaving us alone with a guy who looks no older than me.

He grabs both of us by the arms. Neither of us fights as he leads us to a far corner of the building. He stops by a rusty door, pulling it open with a grunt. "Get in," he commands.

"Get your hands off of me," Emeryn warns. I'm not sure where her moment of bravery came from. She pulls away from his grip.

He pulls a rusty door shut behind him, leaving us alone in the dark room. "You good?" I whisper. "We can stop this at any time."

She sniffs loudly. "No. We have to stop them. We can't let this continue."

I'm not sure how long we've been in the room. The only sounds coming through the metal door are the bellows of ships coming in and out of port. Emeryn hasn't spoken anymore since coming into the room. Her heart rate is elevated, and her stomach is churning.

"Amelia?"

"I'm here," she answers.

"Emeryn isn't doing well. She needs food and water."

"I'll see what I can do." I don't know how much time passes before the rusty door creaks open again.

"Here." The younger man from before hands me a bag of fast food and a bottle of water. "I thought you might be hungry."

"Thank you." I pretend to be terrified. I don't know what Amelia did, but I have no doubt that she was involved in this delivery.

"Is it safe to eat?" Emeryn whispers.

"Yes. It's from my friends."

She takes the bag, rummaging through the wrappers for a few minutes before pulling out a small sandwich. "Tell them, thank you." She devours the hamburger in nearly two bites.

"Get some rest. I'll make sure nothing happens to you." She doesn't argue. She crawls into a ball, pulling her knees to her chest, and lays her head on my thigh. Within minutes, she's asleep.

"Celeste. Are you okay?" a soft voice whispers through the door.

"Jasper?"

"Yeah. I might have knocked the guy out who was guarding the door."

I smile at his words. "My hero," I whisper.

"Are you sure you're okay?"

"You're forgetting what I am. I'm fine. It's Emeryn I'm worried about."

"I'm not forgetting anything. Yes, you're a vampire, but you're the most important person in my life. I don't know what I'd do if something happened to you." Butterflies take flight in my stomach at the words of a werewolf, whispered through a metal door.

"Does Amelia know you're in here?"

He scoffs. "No. She's kind of mean. I snuck in."

I laugh out loud, covering my mouth to mute the sound. "She didn't start out that way. Being a were-wolf-vampire hybrid can do that to a person."

"The sun is rising. Amelia says their contact is supposed to be here this morning. They plan to take the Bandit down." His voice is softer than before. "I need to go."

I hear him scuffle as he moves away from the door. "Jasper. You're important to me, too." The sound of his fingers sliding down the door echoes through the room.

I've lost track of time, so I have no idea how much time has passed when the door creaks open again. "Get up," a man I don't recognize demands. Emeryn startles awake at his command. He reaches down, pulling her arm. "I said, get up."

"Give her time. She's been through a lot." He raises

his hand, swinging it toward my cheek. Against every fiber of my being, I let his hand make contact. "Did that make you feel strong and tough?" I smile a wicked smile.

He doesn't respond. Instead, pulls both of us to standing. "You smell."

"Look who's talking, asshole." Emeryn's spunk is back. He raises a hand, ready to slap her face.

"Do it, and you will not have an arm afterward." The tone of my voice convinces him to stop. He turns, pulling us with him. He drags us to an awaiting car, throwing us into the backseat.

"Put your seatbelt on." He slides into the driver's seat.

"Seems strange that you treat us like shit but want us to strap in for safety. What do you think, Celeste?"

"Protecting the investment," the man answers. "I don't get paid for dead girls."

"I could see how that could be an issue," I answer.

"We're behind you," Amelia says through my mind.

"Everyone?"

"Jasper's here if that's what you're asking."

The car stops in front of an older home in the Garden District. I never spent much time in the city when Viktor was alive, so I don't recognize the street we're on. The driver is at our door seconds later. He doesn't bother to speak this time. He grabs Emeryn's arm, pulling her out of the car. I follow behind as we walk up the perfectly manicured path toward the front door. Several loud bangs on the door later, an older woman opens it, peering through the opening. Her shoulders are slumped, and she's slightly bent at the waist.

"He's in the office," she says, opening the door wide enough for all of us to enter. "They smell."

"You'd smell too if you had to sit in your own piss for twenty-four hours." Emeryn glares at the woman as we pass. "Why don't you come and wipe my ass for me…"

The woman slaps her across the face with enough force to knock Emeryn back a few feet. She's stronger than she looks. "Wait out here," she demands of the two of us and leads our friend into an office off of the foyer. The pocket doors slide closed behind them.

"Celeste? I need an update on what's going on in there."

"The driver went into an office to meet with someone. I'm guessing it's Bandit."

Amelia's sigh echoes through my brain. *"We're having a bit of difficulty out here."*

"Jasper?"

"No, he's fine." She pauses. *"The house is warded, and we can't get through."*

"What the hell do you mean, the house is warded? Who owns this place?"

"I think the better term would be—what…"

"Amelia, just tell me what's going on. I'm not good at riddles."

She clears her throat. *"This home is owned by a very powerful voodoo priestess."*

"Like Ophelia?"

"Stronger."

I close my eyes with her words.

"What?" Emeryn asks, sensing my turmoil. "Something's wrong."

I plaster a fake smile across my face. "No, everything's fine. Stay strong. You're doing so good."

The pocket doors open, and the driver steps in front of us. He slides a thick envelope into his pocket before grabbing each of our arms and pulling us into the office. The desk chair is facing backward, making it impossible to see this asshole they call Bandit. "Have a seat, ladies," a deep voice says, hidden by the chair.

"I'd rather stand," I answer.

The chair turns and the person sitting there knocks both Emeryn and I both for a loop. "I said sit down, Celeste."

"Oh, my God. You're...you're Bandit?" Emeryn asks.

"One of my many names. It's good to see you two again. I hoped it wouldn't come to this, but alas, Celeste didn't follow the rules."

"Fuck you, Drake."

"Tsk, tsk, tsk. Such filthy language from such an innocent young lady. After all, you're only five years old."

"I haven't broken the rules. I haven't killed anyone," I retort.

"Ah, Celeste. The night is still young." He stands, moving in front of us. "See, I can sense it in you now. You want to rip my head from my body and watch as the blood drains slowly onto the designer rug."

"The thought has crossed my mind," I answer.

"Celeste, what is he talking about?"

Drake laughs maniacally. "Your roomie here is a vampire. A very old vampire who made a deal with the devil, per se."

"You're the devil?" she asks.

"Not officially, but we're on a first-name basis."

I'm off the chair and have him backed against the shelves behind him before he realizes I've moved.

"Celeste, no!"

what are you?

I FREEZE IN PLACE, pushing my entire body weight into Drake. *"Don't do whatever you're about to do. I can sense it in you. Whoever the Bandit is, isn't worth it!"* Amelia is screaming through my mind. She's right about one thing, Drake isn't worth it. I back away slowly.

He takes a minute to straighten his sports coat and bow tie. "That's what I thought. All bark and no bite. Oh, wait. I have you mixed up with those useless wolves."

"Drake, what happened to you?" Tears fill Emeryn's eyes as she speaks. "We were friends."

"We were never friends. Although, I think I'd played my part rather convincingly. Maybe in my next life, I'll pursue an opportunity in theater." He turns toward the older woman who hasn't moved since delivering us.

"Take them to their rooms and see that they shower." The woman grabs our wrists, pulling us behind her. She's stronger than a normal human, and I resist the urge to fight. "Remember, Celeste. If you break the rules, you won't be the only one that will suffer." He nods toward Emeryn, saying more with his eyes than his mouth.

"Understood." I reluctantly follow the woman upstairs. She stops in front of a door at the end of the hall.

"This is your room," she shoves Emeryn toward the closed door.

"Celeste?"

"We'll stay together," I interrupt. I don't know what Drake is planning, and I certainly don't trust him enough to leave Emeryn unprotected.

"No, you won't. You will be housed separately," she demands.

This is where I draw the line. I turn toward my captive, looking her in the eyes. I push every bit of my power into forcing her to do my will. "After bringing us upstairs, you've decided that separating us isn't in your best interest. We will serve you better if we're placed together."

The woman's eyes dilate slightly but return to normal much faster than they should. A wicked smile covers her face as she looks between the two of us. "Many vampires, stronger than you, have tried over the centuries to convince me to do their bidding. Just like you, they failed." She opens the door and throws Emeryn inside. Slamming the door behind her.

"Celeste!" Emeryn screams through the closed door.

"You'll be alright," I try to comfort her. Turning toward the older woman. "What the hell is wrong with you? She's terrified."

"She should be." She grabs my arm, pulling me to a closed door several rooms down. "This is your room. Get inside."

"What are you?"

A wicked smile covers her face. "Someone you don't want to mess with. You vampires and wolves are all the same with your delusions of power and authority. You're nothing but a blood-sucking bag of bones." She opens the door, pushing me inside. "Take a shower. You smell like shit."

The door slams behind me, leaving me alone in a lavishly decorated bedroom. Ancient tapestries cover the walls, depicting battle scenes between what appears to be demons and angels. The one hanging above the fireplace is an image of Lucifer's fall from heaven, along with the angels that fell with him.

An oversized four-poster bed sits opposite the marble fireplace and is covered in lavish silk fabric. The furniture reminds me of a time long ago when I was still human. "Who are these people?" I whisper to no one.

This is more than trafficking. *"Amelia?"*

"We're here. As far as we can get, at least."

"What is this place?"

She sighs deeply through my mind. *"We don't know. We can't find any information on the owner of the home."*

"The Bandit is Drake."

"Drake who?"

"My friend from school. Drake Overstreet. I've already researched him and discovered information that dated back over the past hundred years."

"Celeste, why are you just now telling me this?"

I scoff. *"In case you haven't noticed, I've been a little busy."*

"Is he a vampire?"

"No. I would've picked up on that. We've been friends since the first day I was at Ravenwood. The first day we met, a weird sort of electrical shock passed between us when he touched me, but other than that, I didn't notice anything else until the dance."

"An electrical shock?"

I shrug. *"I didn't think anything about it. I figured it was static."*

"Tell me what happened at the dance," Amelia asks.

"Jasper and I were dancing. Drake asked to dance with me, which Jasper obliged. While we were dancing, he called me a slut and said I could do better than a wolf. He knew what I was and told me to not forget the rules, and then he left."

"What the hell, Celeste? What rules?"

"The rules that accompany me not being a five-year-old anymore."

"If he knew about the rules, he must be somehow involved with the voodoo priestess who performed the spell."

"Agreed, except she's not here, and he is. Along with an old woman who just told me that vampires and werewolves were nothing more than blood-sucking bags of bones with delusions of authority."

"Holy shit," she answers. *"What does that mean?"*

"It means she and Drake are neither lycan nor vampire, yet very powerful. I tried to compel her into putting Emeryn and me in the same room. It didn't work."

"Are you two okay for now?"

"I don't know. I think so, but I have no idea what's going on with Emeryn. She's freaking out, and I'm not there to protect her."

"Okay. Let me do some research. We'll figure this out, Celeste. Stay safe, and don't do anything rash."

I scoff at the thought of murdering Drake. *"As time dwindles, that is going to get more and more difficult to promise."*

"Fran is here."

"What? Don't let her get mixed up in this mess. You two are the only family I have left."

There's a noticeable pause before she answers. *"I'll keep her safe. Pinky promise."*

I move into the en suite bathroom, finding every possible item needed to "freshen up." Instead of following directions and showering, I relish the fact that I smell like human excrement and move toward the hallway door. Turning the knob, I pull, expecting the door to tear from the hinges and open. Surprisingly, nothing happens. The door doesn't budge, even so much as an inch.

I try again, this time using all of my force and again, the door doesn't budge. "Emeryn?" I yell through the wood.

"Celeste!" her faint voice answers. "I can't get out."

"Me neither. Are you okay?"

Sobs overtake her words. "I thought I was strong. I'm not. I'm sorry, Celeste."

"Emeryn, don't you dare give up. We're going to get out of this." I resist saying anything else. No doubt Drake has heard every word we've spoken, and thankfully, she doesn't speak again.

I slide down the wall next to the door, sitting as still as possible. Outside the door, I listen to every creak of the antique wooden floors, every whisp of wind from the air vents, every particle of dust flying through the air. The sounds take over my body, pulling me into their web of confusion. If Drake and the woman are something more powerful than vampires or lycan, that doesn't leave many choices.

A tapestry shifts to my right, pulling my attention toward it. It's a scene of a horde of demons, surrounding what looks to be a burning town. Black rock surrounds them as they work together.

Next to it hangs one with a similar image, this time

showing the faces of the crowd. Most resemble creatures from nightmares, while several look human. A
younger man with dark hair is standing off to the side.
His hair is tied behind his neck with an elaborate
ribbon, and he's dressed in seventeenth-century clothing. His face is covered in a familiar smirk.

I move toward the tapestry, hoping to get a better
look. Oh, my God. The image is Drake. How can that be?
I search the image, looking for clues, finding an older
woman not far behind him. She's wearing a long black
dress with a white apron, and her arms are bound in
front of her. A group of men looks to be pulling her
toward the center of the image.

That's the woman who put us in these rooms. She's
wearing a small cross around her neck as she's being
led to what looks like a stake. In the background are
several small wooden homes and pasture land. I've
seen those homes like this before. Where? The memory
hits me like a ton of bricks. Oh, my God. This is a depic-
tion of Salem, and the woman is about to be burned for
witchcraft.

"*Amelia!*" I yell through our connection. "*The
woman is a witch who was burned at the stake, and Drake
was there. He probably made them do it with some sort of
compulsion or something.*"

"*Celeste, slow down. What are you talking about?*"

"*The room they put me in is covered with tapestries.
One of them is an image from the witch trials in Salem. The
woman being burned at the stake is the same woman who*

put me in this room. Drake is in the background, watching, with the same damn smirk covering his face. I don't know what he is, but he's powerful. I look around the room at the other tapestries.

The one next to the Salem scene shows Drake again. This time, he's dressed slightly more modern, but his face is distorted. Where his eyes should be are empty black circles, and his mouth is contorted, showing sharp teeth. I recognize the image from books I used to earn one of my doctoral degrees. I know in an instant what I'm looking at. *"Amelia, he's a demon."*

I hear Amelia laugh in my mind. *"Celeste, don't take this the wrong way, but there are no such things as demons."*

"Two years ago, you would've laughed if I'd told you vampires and werewolves were real. The world is much bigger than we know."

"Celeste, you can't believe..."

"Nothing else makes sense. The other tapestries in the room contain demonic scenes, full of images of monsters and things that nightmares are made from. There are no other explanations, Amelia. He is a demon. I have no idea how to fight him."

She scoffs. *"Nothing is too powerful to die."*

The handle to my door rattles, and the old woman enters without warning. "I see you still smell like shit. You're wanted downstairs."

"Why?"

"You don't need a reason. Get up, or I'll make you get up."

I stand and point to the tapestry. "This is you, isn't it?"

Her eyes follow my finger, and she stares longer than necessary. "That's from a time long ago. Let's go."

Bony fingers wrap around my arm as she leads me out of the room, past Emeryn's door, and to the top of the stairs.

"What about Emeryn?"

"Her attendance isn't required."

For someone who was burned at the stake, she moves remarkably well. She pulls me down the stairs in record time and leads me into the same study from earlier. This time, Drake's not alone. Standing against the far window is Jackson. He's dressed in a black biker jacket and chaps.

"I believe you two have met," Drake announces as he stands from his desk chair.

"What the hell are you doing here?"

"Protecting my investments." A smirk covers Jackson's face.

"Do you have any idea what he is?" I nod toward my former friend.

Jackson shrugs. "He's the man with a shitload of money. That's all I care about."

"How could you do this? Emeryn was your girlfriend."

He laughs loudly. "God, she's stupid if she thinks for one minute I'd choose her. My mate has been chosen since before birth, precisely the reason *she's* not my girlfriend."

"What about Jasper?"

"What about him?"

"He believes in you. Believes you're better than this. Are you willing to prove him wrong?"

Jackson leans against the bookshelf behind him. "Jasper is lost in his own little make-believe world and will never be anything more than what he is at this moment. He's my brother, that's it."

Drake steps beside Jackson, handing him an envelope full of what I assume is money. "Thank you for your services."

"Let me know when you're ready for more."

"Jackson, do you know who you're dealing with?" I repeat my question from earlier.

"Money." He turns, heading toward the door.

"You'll never be Alpha. You're nothing more than a money-hungry coward who won't survive his first day in power."

He turns his head back toward me. "Whatever makes you feel better, bloodsucker. Tell Jasper I said hello. We all know he's out there with the rest of the idiots that followed you here. If they think they can save you, they're as stupid as Emeryn." He turns toward the door, and I've never wanted to kill anyone more in my life.

"Jackson's leaving the house."

"I know. We saw him."

"They know you're here." I wipe a tear from my cheek. I refuse to show weakness.

"Good. We have no intentions of leaving."

For the first time in my life, I'm scared. I don't know what to do next, and there's no way I'm strong enough to fight a demon. If that's even what he is.

"What's the matter, Celeste? What happened to that big bad vampire girl?" Drake's voice is whiny, mimicking a child's voice. "Too bad Daddy isn't here to rescue you."

"I don't know what you're trying to prove, but you don't have to do this."

"I'm not trying to prove anything. You're nothing more than a blip on my radar." He walks back to his chair. "No, my dear. I'm simply fulfilling a promise I made centuries ago."

"How did you know about the rules?"

He laughs. "I wasn't kidding when I said you made a deal with the devil. Your priestess bargained for her powers, and I granted her the ability."

"What was her bargain?"

Drake leans back in the chair, propping his feet on the desk. "Her life, of course."

"Why me? What makes me special?"

He scoffs. "I've wondered that many times. However, a promise is a promise."

"A promise? Who made you a promise?"

"Ah, now you're asking the right questions." He laces his fingers together. "We're betrothed, my dear."

"What the hell are you talking about?"

"I was promised your hand in marriage many centuries ago. I'm here to collect my debt."

I stare at my former friend. "Are you out of your mind?"

"I can assure you I am perfectly sane."

"You set this entire thing up to trap me into some sort of marriage that you think was promised to you? Viktor would never have agreed to such an absurd thing."

"Who said anything about Viktor? No, Celeste. I was promised your hand in return for saving Penelope's life." His words knock the wind from me. "Your mother sold you to save herself."

"But—I killed her."

Drake laughs. "Oh, the irony. I imagine what that vampire of an English professor would be quite proud."

wedding of a lifetime

"ARE you telling me Penelope is alive?"

"You separated her head from her torso. Even I can't bring her back from that. No, Penelope made her deal with me while still in France, long before she faced her final death."

I stare at the demon in front of me. "France? We left France over five hundred years ago."

"Did I stutter?"

"Why would she do that?"

"Strange what people will do when their life is in the balance. I won't pretend to know the circumstances. At the time, she made a choice. Your mother simply chose her life over yours. However, in her defense, most immortal children don't survive as long as you have. I'm sure she never dreamed this day would come." He pours himself a glass of wine. "How rude of me. I'm sure you're famished. Care for something to eat?"

"No, I'm not hungry," I lie. "Are you a—demon?"

Drake smiles. "Ding...ding. You win the gold star of the day."

"Was this whole trafficking thing just to capture me?"

He drinks his wine in one gulp, pouring himself another. "Don't flatter yourself, my dear. Human trafficking has been my past time for many millennia. It's what pays the bills. That idiot wolf happened to grab the wrong girl, and magically, you showed up with her." He motions to the empty chair in front of his oversized desk. "Why don't you sit? I believe you'll be more comfortable."

"I'm fine," I continue. "You went to college to stalk me?"

"What better way to learn your future mate's ins and outs than by becoming their best friend?"

"We were classmates, nothing more."

He drinks his second glass in one gulp. "Imagine my surprise to discover you were more complicated than I expected."

"I'm glad you approve. Why me? I'm sure a promise of betrothal is an everyday occurrence to someone like you. Why choose me?"

Drake shrugs. "Let's just say I'm partial to redheads."

"I hate to break this to you, but I'm not interested in being betrothed to anyone. Let alone a demon."

He pulls a rolled piece of paper from a desk drawer. Breaking the seal, he opens it, rolling it out for me to read. "What's this?"

"Our contract. Well, Penelope's contract, really." Penelope's signature covers the bottom in perfect penmanship. I read through the contract, which clearly states that as payment for Drake restoring her life, she was promising him my hand in marriage.

"I'm not honoring this contract."

Drake's laugh echoes off the wooden walls. "I'm afraid that's not an option. This isn't a contract between a lending organization and its patron. This is a contract, signed in blood and made to a demon of the underworld. Whether you *choose* to honor the contract is of no concern to me. You simply have no choice."

"There's always a choice."

He sighs deeply. "If that's your wish then you will not survive the night."

"So be it."

"Neither will that hybrid you created nor the child she carries in her womb." Amelia's pregnant?

"You wouldn't do that."

"Don't fool yourself into thinking you know me. You do not. What I will and won't do is something you know nothing of."

"Celeste?"

"I can't talk right now."

"Are you okay? Your energy feels different."

"Tell her there is nothing she can do to save you," Drake interrupts.

My eyes flash to his in an instant. Can he hear our conversation? He smiles knowingly. *"I'm good,"* I answer.

"Good girl." His words are condescending.

"I want them here."

He wrinkles his forehead. "Who?"

"My family. I want them here when we're married."

"I'm afraid that's not possible."

"If they're not here, I will take my own life."

Drake claps his hands. "This is getting comedic. How do you propose you'll do that? You're a vampire. Starving yourself will take at least a century, and your body will regenerate any self-induced injuries. Your pretentiousness is amusing."

"Being trapped in the body of a five-year-old makes one search out and research unusual things. I have the means and the willpower to succeed if necessary."

"Do you think you're important enough for me to be concerned whether you take your life?"

I take a deep breath, praying for wisdom and clear thought. "If you didn't think I was important, you wouldn't have gone through the trouble that you have. You lived the life of a human and attended a university, all in the name of 'getting to know me.' You made sure the priestess would grant my desire to be an adult. You have more invested than you want me to believe. I want to know why."

"I will consider your request." He dismisses me with his words.

I refuse to back down. "It's not a request. I will not marry you without them, and I will not marry you here, at this house."

"You're in no position to demand anything."

"Your choice." I look him straight in the eyes, refusing to flinch.

Drake smirks, without releasing my eyes. "Very well."

I turn, leaving him in the office alone. The old witch is waiting by the door and reaches for my arm as I exit. "Touch me, and I'll rip your arm off," I warn.

"That's better." She scoffs as she follows me up the stairs to my room.

"Why do you do his bidding?" I ask as I step inside.

"There is more to every story than what appears on tapestries." She turns, heading down the hallway before stopping in front of Emeryn's door. "She's had a shower, clean clothes, and a hot meal. I believe she's sleeping peacefully at the moment."

"What's your name?"

The woman doesn't look up with her answer. "Miriam." She's down the stairs and out of sight within seconds.

"Thank you, Miriam," I whisper toward her.

I take time to study each of the tapestries, finding

images of Drake in each. Always standing in the background, wearing the same smirk throughout. I wonder if Viktor knew of demons? If so, he never mentioned them. Thoughts of mine and Drake's conversation play through my mind. I have no doubt Penelope would trade my hand in marriage for her survival. I should've killed her centuries earlier. Think of the heartache I would've saved for so many people.

After stripping the bed, for what reason I don't know, and finding nothing unusual, I climb on top and sulk. Viktor had all the answers. He was the strength that kept me alive and learning for so many years. "Daddy, I miss you!" I whisper for no one but me.

Memories of his death flash to mind as images of his body separating from his head and slowly collapsing to the concrete floor flash to mind. I wipe the tears the memory brings from my cheeks. He taught me to never give up, that there's always a way out, and that every person and every creature has a weakness.

"What's going on?" Amelia asks through our connection.

I laugh. *"Just feeling sorry for myself."* I suddenly remember Drake can hear our conversations. *"Amelia, I need you to listen to me without interruption."*

"Okay..."

"Penelope made a deal with Drake centuries ago that promised my hand in marriage in return for saving her life. I don't know any details, so please don't ask."

"Celeste, that can't be legit."

"It is. I thought you weren't going to interrupt?" I hear an exasperated sigh in the back of my mind. *"I've seen the sealed paper and recognized Penelope's signature. I told him I wouldn't honor the marriage without my family there."*

"That's ins..."

"Amelia. Don't respond. I need you to listen very carefully to what I'm about to say." I pause giving her time to put the puzzle pieces together.

"I understand."

"The night that Harrison died, do you remember when he knocked on the door and pretended to be Violet?"

"Yes," she whispers.

"This is like that night. Don't believe everything you see or hear." Amelia is quiet. No doubt trying to figure out if I'm speaking in code.

"Celeste, I don't understand."

"This will be my last time speaking through our connection. I love you."

"Celeste? Celeste! What the hell, Celeste?"

I close our connection and hold the sobs deep inside. I refuse to let Drake know the pain I'm feeling. A knock on the door pulls me back to the present.

"Miriam?"

The door opens slowly and instead of Miriam, Drake is standing in the door frame. He's wearing a black tuxedo with tails, straight from the eighteenth century. "Sorry to disappoint you, my dear."

"I'm not your dear."

"You were wise to cut off communication with them."

I stand, moving toward my former friend and channeling his energy from earlier. "Don't confuse the fact that I cut off communication with the fact that I will marry you in this house without them here. You will not control me."

Drake smirks. "There she is. That's the creature that drew me to the university. Your spunk and fortitude are a combination rarely seen these days. For that reason, I will honor your request." He moves toward an ancient wardrobe in the corner of the room. A wedding dress, matching the age of his tuxedo, spills through the door as he opens it. "We will be married at midnight. Take a shower, and get dressed."

"There's no clock in here. How will I know what time it is?"

"You'll know. We'll leave thirty minutes early, and your friends will meet us there."

I step even closer. "I will not go through with the ceremony if they're not *all* in attendance."

"I have no control over whether they choose to attend."

"I think you do." I close the door in his face, and his laugh pierces the thick door. Even I'm disgusted by the way I smell. I take a shower, grateful for the hot water and overload of bath products. I take more time than usual, making sure every curl is in place, and my makeup is flawless. God, I look just like Penelope and remarkably like Amelia. Opening the bathroom door, I startle to see Miriam standing next to the wardrobe.

"I'm here to help you get dressed."

"I don't need any help."

She laughs. "Even vampires need help buttoning fifty buttons on their back." She pulls the dress out, turning it for me to see a line of buttons extending from the collar to below the waist. It pangs me to admit that she's right. It takes longer than expected for her to button me inside. I step away, turning toward the full-length mirror. The dress hugs every curve and makes me look older than my new body really is. "You look beautiful," she whispers from behind.

"Miriam, why do you serve the demon responsible for burning you at the stake?"

She's so quiet, I don't think she's going to answer. "Before death, I made a deal to serve him for eternity." Her eyes look sad.

"I can help you."

"No, you can't. It's time to go." She leads me out of the room and down the stairs.

"Celeste?" Emeryn's voice instantly turns to tears when she sees me. She's wearing a dress from the same era as my wedding dress, and her hair is pulled into a tight bun behind her neck. She rushes me, pulling me close.

"Are you okay?" I ask, pulling away from our hug.

She wipes a tear. "Yes." She looks around the room. "What is this? Are you wearing a wedding dress?"

"We're getting hitched," Drake says, coming into the room. He turns toward me. "You look lovely." He's still wearing the tuxedo from earlier.

"Drake? What are you talking about?" Emeryn asks.

"My mother made a deal with him and bargained my hand in marriage for her life."

She turns back toward Drake. "What are you?"

"That's the million-dollar question," he answers. "In your world, I'm called a demon. In my world, I'm called a god."

"i don't"

WE'RE USHERED into the back of a modern limousine and driven out of the city toward the marshes and the gulf. I haven't spoken since leaving the house, while Emeryn has asked a ton of questions, none of which are being answered.

"Where are we going?" Emeryn's latest question flies from her mouth.

"It seems you're not going to shut up until I answer. We're going to the wedding location," Drake finally answers.

"We're heading into the middle of nowhere," she argues.

"To a human, it may look that way." He doesn't offer any other information.

My head feels like it's about to explode. Without thinking, I rub my temples, hoping to ease the pain.

Miriam catches my eye and smirks. Is she why my head is hurting? What the hell?

"What's wrong?" Drake asks.

"Nothing. Just missing my family."

He raises his eyebrows, clearly not believing me. "They'll be here."

"I can't see anything," Emeryn continues. "It's too dark. Who gets married in the dark?"

"Shut up." Drake's had enough of her incessant talking.

"Sorry, I'm nervous. I talk a lot when I'm nervous."

"Yay, for us," he answers sarcastically.

I take her hand into mine, hoping the connection will settle her down. She squeezes and stops talking. As the car pulls to a stop, the headlights shine off of an ancient wooden church. "Is this a church?" Emeryn asks.

Drake doesn't respond as someone opens his door. "Stay inside," he warns, leaving us alone. Miriam continues to stare at me, and my head aches more than before. She slides a finger to her mouth, flashing a warning before handing me a folded piece of paper out of sight of Emeryn.

"Let's go," Drake announces, sticking his head back into the car.

"Where's my family?"

"Inside."

Emeryn slides out of the seat first, followed by Miriam. As she steps out, she trips, landing face-first in front of Drake. I don't waste a minute, reading the hastily scribbled words on the palmed piece of paper.

I've blocked your mind. He can't hear when you speak to her.

"Get up, clumsy witch," Drake warns Miriam.

"I'm sorry, master. I don't know what happened. Please forgive me." He pushes her out of the way, reaching his hand in for me. Reluctantly, I take it and step out of the car onto the leaf-covered drive.

"Take her inside," Drake orders. Miriam follows directions, ushering Emeryn inside the rundown building. He holds his arm out to me. "Ready, my dear?"

"No," I answer truthfully, making him snicker. As we walk, I open my mind back to Amelia and am immediately met with her screaming my name.

"I'm here!" I shout back. I look at Drake, wondering if he hears our words. He returns the look and smiles.

"Where are you?" she asks. Her voice is more frantic than I've heard before.

"At a church, preparing for the wedding. Are you here?"

"Dammit. Of course, he sent us to the wrong place. Can you send me some sort of location beacon where I can locate you?"

"Close your eyes, and follow our connection."

She's quiet for a long while as we continue walking. "I don't see them."

He looks around. "They should be here by now. Maybe they misunderstood the directions."

"Maybe they received the *wrong* directions."

"What would I gain by sending them to the wrong place?"

I stop walking. "I don't even pretend to know why you're doing any of this. Nothing can be gained by our marriage. I can't bear you a horde of baby demon-vampire hybrids. I have money, but I imagine money isn't an issue for you."

"Are those the only reasons why you think I'd take you to be my wife?"

I shrug, hoping to stall him in whatever is about to happen. "Our marriage is much more than a monetary or even a future heir situation. No, Celeste. Our marriage will ensure the combination of our two communities."

"What?"

"Are my words not clear?"

"You're marrying a vampire so the vampire and demon worlds will work together? That's your master plan? The vampire world isn't going to give a shit if I'm married to a demon or not. In fact, they'll probably kill me for such an atrocity." I laugh loudly.

"I'm glad I amuse you. There is more to our worlds than you could ever imagine. Your lack of knowledge is comedic." He grabs my arm, pulling me into the building. Miriam is standing behind a makeshift altar. Lit candles surround the room, filling the room with dancing shadows.

"Amelia, I need an ETA. This is getting serious quickly."
"Almost there. Stall."

"Get on with it," Drake demands.

"No." I pull away from his grip. "I told you I will not marry you without my family here."

He sighs. "They're not coming, Celeste. They don't love you. I'm your family now. Miriam, begin the ceremony."

I move faster than mortal eyes can track away from the altar and to the back of the room. Drake is right on my heels. "Not until they're here," I repeat.

"Whatever you think you're about to do, don't," he warns. "You can't outrun me. You are mine, and we will be joined as one. Accept your fate, Celeste. It'll be easier that way."

I pull a small vial from the bust of the gown. "I'd rather die than be married to you."

Drake laughs. "I'm not going to lie. That hurt my feelings a little." His voice is full of sarcasm as he covers his heart and pretends to be injured. "That poison you're holding won't kill you, Celeste. You're a fucking vampire. You're already dead."

"You're right. Normal poison wouldn't affect me. However, this poison isn't normal."

He grabs my hand, trying to force the vial from my grip. My teeth appear, and I feel my appearance change into the creature I've hidden for so long. Emeryn screams, drawing my attention back to the situation.

"Oh, the irony. If you kill me, which you can't, you'll be five years old again. I hope you appreciate this entire situation."

I pop the lid off the vial, bringing it to my lips. *"We're here!"* I lower it in response to Amelia's words as my features return to normal.

He grabs my arm, knocking the vial away. I stare in horror as it seeps through the wooden floorboards. "I'm through playing games," he spews, pulling me toward Miriam. Emeryn is in full-fledged hysterics as she watches the spectacle unfold in front of her.

"Celeste, I'm so sorry," she cries.

"Oh, shut up, Emeryn. No wonder that wolf sold you. All you do is whine."

A howl in the distance lifts my spirits and energy. "Sounds like they're here." He laughs. "Miriam, perform the ceremony."

Miriam wraps an arm around Emeryn and pulls her close. Candlelight flashes off the edge of a blade as she raises it to Emeryn's throat.

"No!" I yell as the blade slices across her neck. The smell of blood fills the room as Miriam slowly lowers Emeryn's body to the floor below. "You bastard!" I scream, rushing to my dying roommate's side. She's clinging to her throat as blood covers her hands and body. Her eyes frantically search the room, looking for answers.

"Emeryn, I'm so sorry. I can help you, but I won't do it without your permission." Her eyes are wild with terror. "Do you want me to turn you?" She nods her head as I grab her arm to drain the blood from her body.

"What do you think you're doing?" Drake interrupts, wrapping his arm around my chest, and pulling me away from my dying friend. "She's not important right now. What matters is our wedding." I fight against his tight muscles without success. For the first time that I can remember, someone or something is stronger than me.

I watch in horror as Miriam collects the blood pouring from Emeryn's neck into a wooden bowl. The entire scene plays before me in slow motion. Drake releases his hold as Miriam fills the bowl.

Staring at the spectacle in front of me brings the part of me to the surface I've kept hidden. One look at my hands shows me they've turned from the hands of an eighteen-year-old to that of a monster. I feel my face lose its soft features, transforming into a creature from nightmares. My body transforms into the predator I am.

"I'm sorry, vampire," Miriam says as I stalk toward her. "I had no choice."

"Celeste, stop!" Amelia's voice is nothing more than background noise as I continue moving toward the murderer. Drake turns the moment Amelia enters the room. She moves at vampire speed and lands between me and Miriam, blocking the witch from me.

"Stop, Celeste. You will lose this body if you kill her." She grabs Miriam and has her out of the building before I register the movement. I turn in the direction of her escape to see three monster-sized wolves and three vampires standing at the entrance of the church. At their sight, the monster inside of me retreats.

"Oh, look, honey. Your family has arrived." Drake motions toward the crew. "So nice of you to come. Please, take a seat."

Amelia appears out of nowhere. "We'd prefer to stand."

"Penelope?" Drake looks confused.

Amelia laughs. "You're not the first one who's thought that over the years."

"The similarity is amazing." He turns back toward me. "The two of you could be twins."

"Celeste is my maker, but I'm sure you already knew that," Amelia answers.

"If this marriage doesn't work out," Drake motions between the two of us, "I'm sure we could work something out." He flashes an evil grin toward Amelia.

The largest of the three wolves growls deeply, resonating through the small room. "Seems my husband isn't a fan of that idea."

Drake walks toward what remains of Emeryn. Her heartbeat is so faint, I can barely hear it. He picks up the bowl containing her blood, dipping his finger inside. "I know you're hungry, my dear." He shoves his bloody finger in my face. The smell fills every pore, making me hunger for something I don't want. "Go ahead. Lick it."

"Celeste, no."

"It seems like your creation has gotten her role in

your life confused. You are the one in charge. You alone hold the power. Not her."

"That's where you're wrong, Drape." Amelia moves closer.

"Drake," he corrects. "My name is Drake." He rolls his eyes at her words. "I take it back. I don't feel that we're compatible."

"I know what you are," she persists.

"Congratulations. Everyone knows what I am. I am pride. I am greed. I am lust. I am envy. I am gluttony. I am wrath. And I am sloth. I am what makes this miserable world habitable."

"You're overly zealous of your importance in this world. Truth is, you're no more than a demon, cast from the pits of hell and forced to live among the humans on Earth."

Drake laughs. "Forced to live among the humans? I choose to live here. Why would I want to live in hell when I can live here?"

"*She's dying,*" I send to Amelia. Emeryn's heartbeat is barely audible, even for me. Amelia transforms into a bright red wolf, nearly as large as her mate. Drake moves away from Emeryn and closer to the ones threatening him. I take advantage of his movement and grab my roommate, pulling her to the back corner of the room. I haven't eaten in days, and her blood is intoxicating.

Behind me, a battle begins as I fight a battle of my own. The hunger that is overtaking my body is almost more than I can handle. Emeryn is unconscious, and her heartbeat is barely a flutter. If I don't act now, she'll die. I close my eyes and hold my nose as I bite into my arm, forcing the flowing blood into her mouth. Emeryn coughs as the blood flows down her throat. "That's it, drink."

I turn toward the fight behind me. Drake is holding his own against the group of mythological creatures. I stand, moving toward the fight when the smallest of the wolves steps in front of me, blocking my path. "Jasper, I'm okay." He nudges his head into my neck and licks my ear before pushing me back against a wall, trying to keep me away from the battle.

The door to the building bursts open as the fight spills into the night. His blue eyes catch mine, and he whines softly. "Go. I'll be fine." His eyes squint, staring into mine. "I won't do anything dumb. I promise." Jasper turns, leaving me alone in the room with Emeryn. Her heart rate has sped up since giving her my blood, which means she's turning.

I carry her lifeless body to the limo. Miriam cowers in the floorboard the moment I open the door. "I...I had no choice," her words are no louder than a whisper. "If I hadn't sliced her neck, Drake would've known I blocked him from your thoughts. That would've ended much worse."

"She drank my blood."

"I understand. Go, help your friends." I stare at the

witch, issuing a silent warning. "I won't hurt her. You have my word."

"Protect her with your life, or I will take yours."

"To be clear, Celeste, I'm helping you because I want to be away from Drake. No matter how much you try to convince yourself otherwise, you are not strong enough to kill me. I will keep her alive because I owe her that. Nothing more, nothing less."

I close the door and turn toward the sounds of the fight. Standing on the bank of the marsh, I watch the battle taking place in front of me. Drake moves just as fast, if not faster than, the creatures he's battling. He's holding his own against the small group of other-worldly creatures.

"What can I do?" I ask Amelia.

"Stay safe," she answers quickly.

I stayed safe my entire life. I'll be damned if I stand by and watch my friends fight for both my life and theirs.

Running full speed toward the battle, I move so quietly that even Drake is unaware of my presence. I move to Oliver's side, finding him not far from the church.

"Celeste. You shouldn't be here." He's breathing heavily.

"Neither should you," I retort. "None of you need to die because of me."

"I can assure you no one is planning on dying today. You need to get back to Emeryn."

I shake my head. "She's safe for now. My place is here."

"Then you should hide. Sacrificing your life for his is not the answer." Oliver moves, leaving me to watch the battle alone.

"Amelia, how can we defeat him?"

"Holy water," she answers quickly. *"I brought two bottles with me. Violet has them."*

A vampire is holding the holy water. "Violet?" I yell, not caring if Drake hears me.

"What the hell are you doing?" I ignore Amelia and continue calling for Violet.

"Here!" she calls, not far from me. I move toward her voice, finding her hiding behind a large tree. "Are you okay?" she asks, looking me up and down.

"I'm good. I need the holy water." She reaches into her pocket, pulling one bottle out. "Shit. The other must have fallen out." I take the bottle at the same time an arm reaches around my throat tightly, pulling me backward.

"Hello, darling. So nice of you to come and join our little post-wedding party." Amelia, Jasper, and Topher are in front of us in an instant.

"Leave her alone," Violet warns.

"Or else?" Drake asks. "I would've thought by now, you all would have figured out this battle is pointless. In fact, I'm rather bored. I'll admit it was fun for a while, but it's time for us to take our leave." He moves backward, pulling me further away from the people I love. Drake's body shivers as a pair of black wings extends from his shoulders. In any other situation, they would be beautiful. In this, they're terrifying. His wings expand six feet on either side of us as he flaps them, lifting the two of us into the sky.

"Celeste!" Jasper's voice is the last I hear as Drake wraps both arms around my waist and lifts me away from the marsh.

"I always love an evening flight. The air is free of filthy humans, and I can be the real me."

"The real you is a demon."

"Are you just now coming to that realization?" His chest rumbles as he laughs at my words.

Viktor could fly. Before the city was so overpopulated, he would take me on short trips over the lake and through the swamps. The height doesn't scare me, but the loss of control does.

"What a lovely way to start our honeymoon," his words echo through the night sky.

"We're not married, Drake."

"The moment blood was spilled on our behalf, you became mine, for eternity."

"I'll never be yours."

Drake's chest rumbles for a second time. "Eternity is a long time. Many things will happen during that time."

"Aren't you worried someone is going to see you?"

"It's New Orleans. A man flying through the sky is nothing more than drunken ramblings."

"You're insane," I spew.

"One of my many strengths." He moves lower in the sky as we approach the river. "Look at them down there. Stupid humans, working their nine-to-five jobs, making money for someone else."

"Humans aren't stupid. They're resourceful, resilient, and alive. That's more than I can say for you."

Drake scoffs. "They are nothing more than a bag of bones, whining all the time. I've lived among them long enough to know."

"You're weak," I spew. "You're nothing more than a jealous egomaniac who feels like he has to prove to everyone how big and bad he is."

"Don't fool yourself, wife. I'm more powerful than anyone you have ever known. I have no one to be jealous of."

The holy water Violet handed me is still squeezed tightly in my hand. I slowly wiggle my arm free of his grip just as we cross the river. If I'm going to try this, I'm running out of time. If we enter the Quarter, thousands of people will have the story of a lifetime. It's now or never.

Sliding the lid off slowly, I throw the contents over my head, splashing Drake directly in the face. He screams and simultaneously releases his grip around my waist. I put every bit of energy into copying the motions I watched my father perform so many times and slowing my descent toward the unforgiving earth. Turning my body prostrate to the ground, I land gracefully on the banks of the Mississippi River with Drake landing in front of me. The skin on his face is loosely hanging from the bone. One of his eyeballs is dangling from the socket, and the cartilage in his nose is completely exposed. "That wasn't nice, sweetheart." His words are slurred and angry.

I move faster than he can track with one working eye, knocking his legs out from underneath him. He hits the ground with a loud thud and is back on his feet seconds later. He swings an arm in front of him in the opposite direction of where I'm standing.

I move again, this time, shoving him from behind. Drake hits the ground face-first and is back up quickly, swinging toward empty air. His movements confirm my suspicion. He can't see. The holy water took his eyesight. Armed with that knowledge, I repeat the assault on his unsuspecting body, knocking him into trees, river water, and anything close enough to cause damage to his already hurting body.

"Having trouble, dear?" I mock his tone from earlier.

"Nothing that won't be fixed momentarily." His wings extend to either side of him as he tries to lift into the sky. One of his wings is covered in holes from splashes of water.

"It's hard to believe that a tiny bottle of water, blessed by a bag of bones, could do this much damage to such a *powerful creature*," I mock his words from earlier.

"You're still not powerful enough to kill me." He laughs. "Even if you were, you won't risk returning to the helpless child you once were."

I move behind him, locking his neck in place. "Don't count on that. I found someone to perform a spell twice. Finding another won't be difficult."

He turns faster than I can track, wrapping both arms around mine and locking me into place. His face has already begun healing, and from the look in his eyes, his sight is returning. "Anyone ever tell you that you talk too much? You should've taken the opportunity when you had it." I plant my feet, refusing to move backward any further. "You will be punished for this." He leans, planting his lips squarely on mine, and kisses me. His tongue pushes through my lips, forcing them open. I bite with every bit of force I have, taking the end of his tongue into my mouth.

"Bitch!" he spews as blood spills from the corner of his mouth. I spit the tip of his tongue at his feet. "I will make sure your punishment is painful and lengthy."

"Fuck you."

"Oh, that will be happening, too. Many, many, many times." Movement behind him catches my eye as I catch a glimpse of red fur moving quickly.

"I will never give myself to you." I keep his attention on me.

"I like it better when they fight, anyway. You should prove to be quite fun." He stretches his wings out again. The holes that were there earlier are gone, and his wing is back to normal. "Ready to go home and consummate this marriage?"

Drake screams in an ear-piercing pitch as his wings ignite in flames. Amelia moves toward him in human form and vampire fangs bared. She's holding a water bottle full of what I assume is holy water. Drake falls to the ground, writhing in pain.

I straddle his hips, turning back into the creature I keep hidden, and bite into his neck. The warmth of the fluid entering my body satiates a thirst that has begged to be fed for years. He screams in agony as I drain his body of nearly every ounce of blood.

Does all blood taste this good, or is demon blood special? Questions spiral through my mind as a haze covers the world surrounding me. "Celeste!" I hear my name being called from somewhere else. "Celeste! Stop! Don't kill him."

Someone is pulling me, trying to force me away from heaven. "Celeste, stop!" Drake's heartbeat is no louder than a soft thump as I continue my assault. Strong arms wrap around me as teeth latch onto my shoulder, bringing me back to reality and forcing me to release my hold on Drake's neck. I turn, ready to kill whoever separated me from the blood, and see two familiar blue eyes.

"Jasper?"

"Stop, Celeste. I need you."

My breathing regulates as the blood-induced fog lifts from my brain. Oh, my God. What did I do?

"He's still alive," Topher says.

"Not for long," Xavier announces. "Celeste nearly drained him dry."

Amelia picks up what remains of Drake's body, separating his head from his body in one quick swipe. "There. I killed Drake," she announces, throwing the lifeless body to the ground. "Did you hear that, universe? It was me, not Celeste!"

"I don't think that's how it works." My voice is no louder than a whisper. Jasper wraps me in his arms, collapsing on the ground with me in his lap. "This is going to be awkward when my body returns to a five-year-old." I laugh, hoping to relieve the tension. We sit, wrapped in each other's arms for what feels like an eternity.

"Celeste, when you killed Tammy, the change was instantaneous. If you were going to change, it would've already happened." Amelia squats to my level.

She's right. Oh, my God. She's right. I pull my hands in front of my face, seeing the hands of an adult. Do I dare to think the rules weren't broken? Jasper pulls away slightly, sliding a loose curl behind my ear. "Everything is going to be okay...you're going to be okay."

I turn, seeing my family covered in mud and half-naked. They risked their lives for me. "Thank you." My words are inadequate.

home, sweet home

TWO HOURS PASS before we move from our spots on the riverbank, and I'm still in the body of an adult. My mind has been everywhere from relief to extreme guilt, all within a short amount of time. A familiar black limousine stops along the bank. Miriam steps in front of me, wrapping her arms around my waist.

"Thank you, Celeste. You have freed me." I stare at the woman in front of me. Her wrinkles are gone, and her face resembles the image in the tapestry from Drake's house. "Emeryn is in the car. She's alive but asleep." She turns, taking a deep breath. "I've always wanted to explore this city. I've heard great things about the French Quarter."

"I don't understand. Were you held captive?"

"In a way, yes. That's all I'm willing to share at the moment." She turns toward our small group. "Thank you, all. I'll forever be in your debt. We are even. Good-bye, Celeste." Miriam erupts into a puff of smoke and disappears before our eyes.

"What the hell was that?" Jasper asks.

"A very powerful witch," Amelia answers.

"I believe she was more than that." Oliver shuffles the burned grass where she stood moments earlier.

"I don't think I want to know," Jasper answers, lacing his fingers through mine. "Let's go home."

Xavier moves in front of his son. "As much as I'd like to do that, this isn't over. Jackson's still out there, and he's a loose cannon."

"What are you suggesting, Dad?"

"I'll take care of Jackson," Topher interrupts.

"I don't want him dead." Xavier's voice is so soft that his words are hard to understand.

"I have no intention of killing him. A little rehabilitation, New Orleans style, might be just what he needs."

Xavier clears his throat. "Thank you, Christopher. He's my son and..."

"I understand. But to be clear, he's not capable now nor will he ever be capable of being the next Alpha of North Mississippi." Topher turns toward Jasper. "Your son will be the heir, just not the one you expected. Jasper, do you accept the decree?"

My heart sinks remembering our conversation by the lake. Jasper doesn't want to be alpha. Now he's left without a choice. He closes his eyes. "I accept and will make you both proud."

"I have no doubt you will."

I squeeze his hand, hoping to offer strength through our connection. He squeezes back, refusing to let go the entire car ride to Viktor's Garden District home. Topher hands the limo driver a wad of money, and the two share a look that warns him never to speak of anything he witnessed tonight.

Oliver lifts Emeryn from the car, taking her inside. Standing on the front walkway, memories flood my mind of the rare times I spent here with my father throughout the years. Before New Orleans became such a tourist attraction, we spent most of our time at this home. I haven't been back since. Most of our time together was spent in the home across the river.

"Are you okay?" Jasper asks, squeezing my fingers tightly.

I sniff loudly. "I am. It's been a while since I've been here. This home holds a lot of memories."

The front door slams open, and a face I haven't seen since August is in front of me in an instant. "Celeste!" Fran exclaims, wrapping her thin arms around my back. "I've missed you so much." She steps away, searching me for any injuries. "Are you alright?"

"I'm fine." I pull her close for another hug. "I've missed you, too."

She looks at the crowd behind me. "I'm still pissed

that you wouldn't let me come," she spits her words at Amelia.

"I know you are, and I don't blame you. In my defense, Celeste demanded that you stay safe."

Fran raises an eyebrow toward me. "It's true. You can be pissed at me," I answer, defending Amelia's actions.

"I'll forgive both of you this time." She smiles, squeezing my shoulders one more time. "Thank goodness you're home." She turns toward Jasper. "Who are you?"

He looks nervous. "I'm Jasper." He reaches a hand toward my nanny. "It's a pleasure to meet you, Ms. Fran."

"You're a lycanthrope?"

"He's the next Alpha of North Mississippi," Amelia answers.

"Well, then come on in, wolf." She pushes his hand away, giving him a big hug.

Entering the stately mansion, I'm surprised to see it looks much like I remember. The furniture has changed over the years, but still in the same style as before.

"This house still gives me the heebie-jeebies," Amelia announces as she and Topher come inside.

"I believe you'll find plenty of rooms, fully stocked with whatever you might need. Please, make yourself at home," Fran offers as Xavier follows them up the stairs.

"Emeryn is in the first room," Oliver announces,

coming down the stairs. "She's asleep and most likely will be for the next few days."

"Your roommate?" Fran asks. "What happened?"

We spend the next few hours going over every detail of the events that led us here, with Fran hanging on every word. While the rest of the lycan retreated upstairs for sleep, Jasper is still at my side. He looks exhausted as he fills in the parts of what happened while I was with Drake.

"Why don't you get some rest?" I ask for his ears only.

"I don't want to leave you alone." He laces his fingers through mine. "I'd rather stay down here with you."

"What if I come with you? I need a shower anyway."

"I need to check on Topher," Amelia announces. "Get some rest, Jasper. You earned it." She stands, moving upstairs. *"Be smart, Celeste."*

"I'm old enough to have sex if I want."

"Yes, you are. Just be smart. You need a shower first...just sayin'. You stink."

I roll my eyes, hoping she can feel the motion as I move upstairs, pulling Jasper behind me. I take him to the top floor of the house, stopping in front of what used to be my father's room.

"Are you alright?"

"This was my father's room." The door is standing open, revealing a large four-poster bed.

"If you'd like some time, I can go..."

"No," I interrupt. "I'll be fine." I pull him to an open room, several doors down. "This was my room." The decor has changed since then and now matches the age of the house. Instead of a child's room, it looks like an ordinary guest room. I open the chest of drawers, finding clothes and undergarments that are my size. "Thank you, Fran," I whisper. "I'm going to take a shower. I can only imagine what I smell like." I turn, not giving him a chance to say anything.

The water feels amazing as it runs down my body. Several shampoo and conditions later, my hair has regained its color. I scrub every part of my body twice, making my skin bright pink and raw. Stepping out of the shower, butterflies take flight in my stomach. Why am I nervous?

I've imagined what sex would be like for years, but now that I'm faced with the possibility, I'm terrified. Suck it up, Celeste. You're a grown woman who can have sex with whoever she wants. I stare at the vampire in the mirror, offering her the pep talk of a lifetime.

I take my time drying off and slip on a pair of super short pajama bottoms and a tank top. Brushing through the tangles, I pull my hair on top of my head, rolling it into a huge bun. I stare at my image in the mirror. My cheeks are flushed from Drake's blood, and my eyes are glowing. For the first time in a while, I feel like an actual adult. Not a kid, masquerading in a strange body.

This is it. The moment I've dreamed of for more

years than I care to count. I take a deep breath and open the door to the sounds of soft snoring. Moving to Jasper's side, I pull the covers over his body, tucking the blanket around him before sliding in on the other side. I move as close as possible, wrapping him inside my hold, and lay my head behind his. I can't sleep, but I can cuddle.

Hours pass, and Jasper hasn't moved a muscle, which is a testament to his exhaustion. Downstairs, the sounds of soft conversations between Violet, Oliver, Amelia, and Fran echo through my ears. They're discussing my future like it's their own.

Fran is worried about me drinking Drake's blood, and Amelia is worried about me in general. Their conversation proves that no matter how old I am or how grown I look, I'm still a child in their minds.

Fingers lacing through mine draw me back to the present. "Celeste?" Jasper's sleepy voice whispers.

"I'm here." His grip tightens as he flips around, facing me.

"I'm glad you are." He slides closer until our lips are inches apart. "You were amazing tonight."

"No, I wasn't. I couldn't save Emeryn."

"You did save her."

I scoff. "I'm not sure becoming a vampire and roaming the earth for all eternity is saving. It's a lonely existence."

"You don't have to be lonely anymore." His eyes

search mine as he glances toward my lips. I don't wait for him to decide what to do. I lean forward, gently placing my lips on his. Our kisses are soft at first, then turn into desperation quickly.

Jasper's hand slides behind my neck, pulling me even closer and not leaving any space between us. I slide my hand under his shirt, and he freezes in place. "What?" I ask.

He pulls away slightly. "This is going to sound crazy."

"Okay."

"I've never done this before," he admits.

"Done what? Kissed a girl?"

"No, been in bed with a girl." His cheeks turn a soft shade of pink. "I'm a virgin, Celeste. I've spent every waking hour trying to keep Jackson alive and out of trouble. I've never had a real girlfriend before."

"Aren't we a good combination?" I laugh, pulling him closer to me. "Maybe we could practice with each other."

Jasper smiles, touching my lips with his. "I'd like that. It may take several practices to get it perfect."

"That's what the old wives' tales say. Practice makes perfect." My hand resumes its position on Jasper's chest, feeling every muscle on his rock-hard stomach. His hand matches mine, lifting the hem of the tank top and sliding his warm hand onto my back.

"Are you sure about this?" He asks between kisses.

"Only if you are," I answer.

"I've been ready since the first night in the bar. Even before I knew what you were, I knew you were the one. You're beautiful, Celeste. Inside and out. I want nothing more than to do this with you now and forever more."

His words stir emotions I've held deep inside. I move until there's not an inch of space between us. I reach to pull the tank top off when an unfamiliar feeling hits me in the stomach. I freeze in place.

"Celeste? What's going on?"

"I don't know." The feeling hits me again, this time pulling at my mind. I've felt the feeling before, but not for years. It's the same feeling I got when Harrison was trying to get into our home and kill Amelia. Oh, my God. I jump out of bed. "Someone is here."

"Who? Drake is dead."

"Celeste? What's going on? Your energy feels weird."

"Get dressed, now!" I bark toward Jasper. He doesn't question me and slides back into the jeans he stripped out of earlier.

"Someone's here." I relay through our connection and hear Amelia curse through my mind as Jasper and I leave our room. I move vampire speed to the bottom floor while he wakes up Xavier and Topher.

"Who's here?" Oliver asks.

"I don't know, but it's something that shouldn't be here."

"Vampire?" Fran asks.

"I don't think so."

"Then what the hell is it?"

"Lycan," Topher answers, landing on the foyer floor.

"Should we be worried?" I ask the Alpha of New Orleans.

He turns, facing Xavier and Jasper. "It's Jackson."

the next alpha

"WHY IS JACKSON HERE? More importantly, *how* did he find us?" Jasper asks the room.

"He's more efficient than we thought," Amelia answers.

"What should we do?" Jasper looks around the room for an answer.

Fran steps forward. "We invite him in, of course. He's not going to try anything in a room full of the most powerful creatures in the South, is he?"

Xavier scoffs. "Depends on the day and what kind of mood he's in."

Fran opens the door to complete blackness. He's out there, I feel it. "If you're going to lurk around my home, I suggest you have the balls to come to the front door." Her words are no louder than normal speech.

A woman is shoved on the porch with Jackson

directly behind her. "Stephanie?" I ask my fellow party planner.

"Celeste?" she cries. Her face is covered in red splotches, and her eyes are bloodshot.

"What's going on, son?" Xavier steps beside Fran.

"Looks like you're having a party without me."

"You caught us. We're living it up in the Big Easy with a vampire and lycan rave. The band should be here any minute," Amelia delivers her sarcasm without a hint of humor.

"Why is Stephanie here?" I ask, hoping to deflate whatever is about to happen.

"Shut up, bitch. This is all your fault."

"What's Celeste's fault, Jackson?" Jasper moves closer to his brother.

"This, man. You. Me. Everything. I'm the rightful Alpha, little brother."

"What are you talking about, son?" Xavier joins Jasper's side. "No one has made any decisions about..."

"Shut up, old man. I'm not as dumb as everyone thinks I am. I know *he* made Jasper Alpha." Jackson points at Topher. "Well guess what, vampire lover. You have no power over me or my pack. They're going to follow me, not you or Jasper."

"That's enough, son. I should've taken care of you long ago. I'm sorry I let it get to this point. You're not mentally well."

Xavier's words seem to affect Jackson. He looks

down, giving me enough time to snatch Stephanie from his grasp. A growl escapes his lips the moment he realizes that she's gone. The terrified girl looks at me in confusion before losing consciousness. "You shouldn't have done that!" He screams, shifting into a wolf right on my front porch.

Before I register what's happened, Jasper has shifted and is on top of his brother. "Jasper!" I scream, following them out the door. They're moving so quickly I can barely track their movements. They look like a ball of fur and teeth as they continue the fight further toward the street.

"We have to do something," I yell toward the audience behind me. "Xavier! They're your children. You have to stop them. They'll kill each other."

Amelia steps beside me. "The true Alpha will win."

"What do you mean? Topher already granted Alpha to Jasper."

"Yes, he did. However, in lycan culture, Jackson just challenged him for the role. Whoever wins is the Alpha. We cannot interfere." Amelia attempts to wrap her arm around my waist.

"What the hell kind of logic is that?" I pull away, moving closer to the duo. "I won't allow this."

"You can't interfere," she reminds me.

"Watch me."

"No." Topher wraps his large hand around my arm. "This is lycan business, not vampire."

"Dammit!" I haven't felt this helpless since being trapped in the body of a child.

"Celeste?" a soft voice calls from the top of the stairs. Just because tonight needed something else thrown in, Emeryn is awake. "I'm hungry," she whispers. Her eyes look crazed, and her face looks sad. "Why am I so hungry? Something smells delicious." She lifts her nose to the sky and the fight outside. Emeryn moves quickly, but without the skills to control her new body, she plummets down the stairwell face first, landing inches from the front door.

"Why the hell is she awake?" Amelia asks, moving to her side. "She should be asleep for the next few days."

"Because her blood was nearly drained," Violet answers, wrapping Emeryn in her arms and pulling her back upstairs. "I'll get her some goat blood. You keep Celeste from doing something stupid." She's talking to Amelia but glaring a silent warning toward me.

"Emeryn, my love." Jackson is standing at the door in human form and nearly naked.

"Where's Jasper?" Xavier asks.

"Oh, settle down, Daddy-O. He's fine. He'll be unconscious for a few hours, but he'll live. He was always the weak one."

"Jackson?" Emeryn turns, facing her captor. "You sold me...to those men...to do horrible things to me."

"Come on. You would've been perfect for them.

Think of all the men you could've kept happy." He smirks, wiping blood from the corner of his lip.

"I trusted you," Emeryn continues. "I loved you."

"Seems you need to be a better judge of character."

"That's enough," Xavier booms. "As your Alpha, I demand that you shut the hell up."

"You're not my Alpha." Jackson moves quickly and is on top of his father in an instant. He slices a hidden weapon across Xavier's throat, cutting him from ear to ear. Jackson puts all of his weight on his father as he fights to breathe. "Now, I'm *your* Alpha."

"I'm so hungry. Why does his blood smell so good?" Emeryn screams as she breaks free from Violet's grip. She's on the floor in front of Xavier's bleeding corpse in a heartbeat. Just as she grabs onto his neck, Oliver wraps his arms around her, pulling her away.

Topher erupts into wolf form, throwing Jackson against the staircase wall. "You can't harm me!" Jackson yells. "I'm Alpha."

"You're no one's Alpha," I spew. "You're nothing more than a psychopathic murderer who doesn't deserve to live."

"Lucky for me, you don't get to make those decisions." I can feel the anger rolling off of Topher as he holds Jackson in place.

"Let him go," a voice orders from the doorway. Jasper's standing in the doorframe and breathing hard. His hair is disheveled and blood drips from his eye and nose.

"Seriously, little brother?" Jackson says with a smirk covering his face. "You learn the hard way, don't you?" Topher backs away, releasing Jackson.

"No. I will not allow this." I step between them. "You've already killed your father. I will not allow any more bloodshed to take place in my home."

"Celeste, you can't inter…"

"Fuck the rules, Amelia. I'm stopping this right now. This is my home. I will not condone a werewolf fight in it." I turn to Jackson. "Go. Before I make you go."

"You can't do anything to me, bloodsucker."

"Do not force me to show you. You are speaking to the oldest vampire in New Orleans, and, as such, I demand your respect. Do not confuse my tolerance with your stupidity as weakness." I move closer to him as I speak. "I will not hesitate to rip your throat from your body before you take a breath."

Jackson has the audacity to laugh. "You can't, can you?" He looks around the room, laughing. "A little birdie told me you'll be a child again if you kill." He looks past me, toward Jasper. "I never thought you'd be into little kids, Jas, but to each his own. I could've gotten you one of your own if I'd have known."

Half a heartbeat later, I have Jackson backed against the same wall where Topher held him moments earlier. "Celeste, no!" Amelia and Jasper say in unison.

"Celeste, no," Jackson mocks their voices. "No, Celeste…" Jackson's voice trails off as blood sprays from his chest. What the hell? I turn, realizing Jasper's standing beside me, holding the butt of a knife he stabbed into his brother's heart.

"Goodbye, brother. I'm sorry I couldn't save you from yourself." Jasper pulls out the knife, wiping the blood on Jackson's shirt as his body slides in slow motion down the wall.

Jasper begins sobbing the moment his brother's body hits the floor. He slides next to him, lifting his head into his lap and smoothing Jackson's messy hair. I don't know what to say. There are no words adequate for what he's feeling. I sit next to him and offer comfort through silence. I once heard someone talk about holding space with someone, and didn't understand the meaning until this moment.

The room empties, leaving the two of us alone with Jasper's dead father and brother. I feel Amelia nearby, but am grateful for the time alone.

Jasper's tears have gone silent as he gently places his brother's head on the floor. "Celeste, I'm so sorry."

I lace my fingers through his. "You don't owe me an apology."

"I killed him." His voice is barely louder than a whisper.

"You didn't have a choice. He killed your father, and you would've been next."

He sniffs loudly. "I spent my entire life trying to save him, and now I'm the one who killed him."

"You did everything you could. This isn't your fault."

Jasper moves to his father's side. "I'm sorry, Dad."

We stay next to his family until the sun begins to rise, filling the room with light. Topher steps into the room, still wearing blood-stained clothes. "It's time to prepare the bodies for transport."

Jasper nods, standing from his spot on the floor. "Lycan tradition is to wrap the bodies in white linen after death. A cremation ceremony will occur at home."

"Tell me how I can help," I say as I stand.

"You've already helped." Jasper leans down, kissing me on the forehead. "Thank you for being here with me."

"Amelia and Fran have the items prepared. We'll take them one at a time," Topher says, moving behind Xavier. "Alpha first." He bends down, lifting the large man like he weighs nothing. We follow them through the swinging door into the kitchen, where the island has been cleared and covered with the off-white fabric.

Fran and I stand out of the way as Topher, Jasper, and Amelia take special care to wrap Xavier's body methodically and ceremoniously in the fabric. They move his body to the garage and the awaiting SUV, then they do the same for Jackson.

Several hours later, the sun is high in the sky, and both bodies have been loaded and are awaiting transport back to Mississippi. "I need to call my mother," Jasper announces from the corner of the kitchen where he retreated. "She needs to know before we show up."

He steps out of the back door with his cell phone in his hands.

"Will he be alright?" I ask the lycan in front of me.

"He will," Topher answers. "It's not easy to become alpha so young, but he has the strength and bloodline to do it."

"He's going to need your help," Amelia adds.

"My help? How can a vampire help?"

"He's not going to need you to be a vampire. He's going to need you to be his support behind the scenes." Amelia wraps her fingers through Topher's as she speaks. "Alpha is a demanding job with not much time for anything else. He's going to need you more than he realizes."

......

Five hours later, our small caravan of cars pulls in front of the quaint blue cottage in Natchez. Jasper's mother is the first one out the door. Her eyes are swollen and red as she meets us next to the SUV.

"I'm sorry, Mama. I tried to save them."

"I know, baby. I know." They stay wrapped in each other's arms, holding each other tightly. "We shouldn't have put the responsibility of your brother on you. That wasn't fair, and I'm sorry."

"I failed him. I failed them both."

Leann pulls away from her son. "You didn't fail anyone, and I don't want to hear those words again.

You're the next Alpha. That means you lead the pack, Jasper. It's what you were born to do. Jackson may have been firstborn, but you're the rightful heir. It was never meant to be Jackson. I see that now. No matter how hard we tried to help him or steer him on the right path, it didn't make any difference." She steps away from her son and lowers her head to him. "I swear my allegiance to you, my Alpha." I wipe a silent tear.

the ceremony

THE NEXT FEW days are a blur of emotion and life. All of the vampires, including Emeryn, are together in the Natchez home that belongs to Amelia. Topher has been gone most of the days, helping the pack get everything suited for the funeral and Jasper's initiation service. With everything that's going on, I haven't seen Jasper since we arrived in town.

> How are u?

My phone buzzes, and I smile at the familiar number.

> I'm doing good. More importantly, how are u?

Jasper waits a few minutes before answering.

I'm gonna be ok. R U coming to the
celebration?

Would it be ok?

I'm not sure a vampire is going to be very welcomed at a lycan initiation.

I'll make sure it is. See u tonight.
Miss u.

Miss u 2.

"Amelia?" I call through our connection.

"Yes, ma'am?" she says, opening the door to my room. "You called?"

"Jasper wants me to go to the ceremony tonight. Will the lycan allow that?"

She huffs a laugh. "They're not given the option of whether Jasper is Alpha. Whatever he says, goes."

"I guess I'm not used to the ways of the lycan. Vampires just do their own thing. They're not really at anyone's beck and call."

"Yeah, it took me a while to get used to it." She covers her stomach and makes a face. "God, I'm so hungry. Before I discovered I was a hybrid, I started drinking more blood than usual. Now I've doubled that and am still hungry. I don't know what's wrong with me."

Drake's words rush back into my brain. With every-thing that's happened, it slipped my mind. "Amelia?"

"Hmm?" she asks, burping slightly.

"You might want to sit down."

Her forehead scrunches at my request, but she walks into the room and sits next to me. "What's up, little one?"

"When I was in New Orleans at Drake's house, he told me something."

"Okay…"

I scratch my arm, not sure how to relay the informa-tion. "Is there…is there a chance you could be pregnant?"

Amelia burst out in laughter. "Pregnant? I'm a vampire."

"True, but you're also half lycan."

She instantly stops laughing. "You think that's why I'm so hungry?"

I nod. "Plus, Drake said you were."

She stands, moving toward the second-story window. "What the hell? I don't know if it's possible, but what if it is? I mean, would it be a vampire or a wolf or—oh, my God— what if it's like Bella's baby and is going to eat me from the inside out?"

I don't know what she's talking about, but the expression on her face makes me smile. "I think a preg-nancy test would be the first step, then we take it from there with the piranha baby."

Amelia sits back on the bed. "Seriously, Celeste. I

never thought being a mother was in my future. I don't know how to feel about this." She turns toward me. "Don't take this the wrong way, but I always felt like you were the only child I would ever have."

"I don't take that the wrong way, at all. I've thought of you as my mother since the first moment we met, and you were wearing that crazy outfit, trying to convince me you were Penelope."

"Do me a favor?" she asks. "Don't mention that again. I don't know how you and Viktor didn't erupt into hysterics when I showed up wearing that." We laugh until tears replace the smiles.

"I love you, Mom," I whisper.

"I love you too, daughter." She pulls away, looking down at her stomach. "Do you think it's possible?"

"I hope so. I've always wanted to be a big sister."

"Let's get ready for tonight. We can grab a test on the way." Amelia stands, leaving me alone in the room. I have no doubt she's pregnant, but I'll let her find out the traditional way. I glance through the closet, hoping to find something I can wear to the lycan celebration. What do people wear to an Alpha initiation?

"Celeste?" A soft knock on my door interrupts my makeup attempt. Emeryn enters my room. She looks beautiful, even more than before the transformation.

"Emeryn! God, you look great. How do you feel?"

She smiles. "I feel...different but good. I haven't had a chance to talk to you since this whole thing happened."

"Yeah, I'm sorry about that. It's been a little hectic."

"Thank you for what you did."

I glance down at her words. "I'm sorry for what happened."

"Yeah, me, too. Look at the bright side, at least I won't age, and we can be roomies for eternity."

I smile, not wanting to go into the explanation of why I'm no longer immortal. "I need you to dress me for this thing tonight. I don't have a clue what to wear."

Emeryn claps her hands together. "That's my favorite thing to do!" She hurries to my closet, searching through the meager amount of clothes inside. Seconds later, she holds a black wide-legged pantsuit in front of her. "There's not a lot to choose from, but this seems to be the lesser of all evils." She lays the outfit on the bed, heads back into the closet, and emerges with a pair of purple heels and a stretchy sequin belt. "These are the icing on the cake." Emeryn motions to a chair in the corner. "Let me see if I can get your makeup in order. Do you mind?"

"God, no. I need help."

She laughs. "You act like you just started wearing makeup."

"You have no idea."

Twenty minutes later, Emeryn steps away from her creation. "Gorgeous," she whispers. "If I do say so myself."

"Ready?" Amelia says, opening my door. She clicks

her tongue when I stand. "Damn, you look good. Those lycan are going to be all over you."

"I'm only interested in one." I smile, turning back to my personal stylist. "Will you be okay here, alone?"

"Yep. Fran's going to be with me, and she scares me a little."

I can't help but laugh. "Don't leave the house for any reason. You're not ready yet."

"I know, Mom," Emeryn answers.

Amelia laughs out loud. "Oh, my God. I can't tell you how many times I've called her that over the past few years. It's good to have a blood sister." The two of them share a fist bump, making me roll my eyes.

"Find a book to read," I say through our new connection.

"What the hell? Was that you? Did you just talk to me in my head?"

"Yes. Because I am your maker, it's something we can do now."

She smiles. "First, I'm not going to read. That's for boring people. Second, you'd better keep me informed of every detail from tonight. Third, have fun."

Violet, Amelia, Oliver, and I pile into the black SUV we used to transport the lycan bodies and head toward the Alpha initiation. I have no idea what to expect when we get there. Oliver and Violet are tagging along, just in case. They plan on staying away from the celebration but close enough that they can respond quickly if we need them.

Oliver pulls the truck to a stop in front of an older warehouse on the outskirts of town. There are barely any cars in the parking lot, but I recognize a familiar truck. Butterflies fill my stomach the minute I spot it.

"Are you sure this is it?" Amelia asks next to me. "It looks like we're about to make a tire or something."

"This is the address Topher sent you," Violet answers. "We checked the site out earlier. It's legit. We're going to be at a diner not far up the road. If anything happens, we can be here in seconds."

"Understood," Amelia answers, sliding out of the other side. We watch as they leave us in the middle of nowhere. "Ready?"

"As I'll ever be," I answer, lacing my fingers through hers.

Topher appears from nowhere. "You two are a sight for sore eyes."

"Is everything okay?" Amelia asks her mate.

"There are a few lycan upset about the change, but they'll get over it. Most of them have pledged their support to Jasper already." He looks at me. "Celeste, you need to be prepared for what you're about to witness. The alpha initiation is..." he pauses, stuck on words. "It's sexual in nature."

"Sexual? What the hell are you talking about, Topher? Is Jasper going to have sex with someone while I watch?"

"No, nothing like that. At least, not usually."

Amelia holds up her hands. "What my husband is

trying to say, but doing a lousy job of, is, traditionally, the initiation is when a mate is bonded to the Alpha."

I stop moving. "Are you two telling me Jasper is going to be bonded to a lycan tonight?" I feel tears immediately flood my eyes.

They share a look. "Maybe not."

"*Maybe* not? Are you fucking kidding me? Why am I here? I don't want to witness that."

Topher sighs. "As the oldest vampire in the region, you need to be here to continue with the joining of our groups. You represent thousands of vampires who will listen to you."

"No one listens to me, Topher. I'm a five-year-old in all of their minds. It wouldn't matter if I were ten thousand years old, I'm never going to be Viktor."

Amelia places a hand on my shoulder. "No one expects you to be Viktor. But Topher's right. You represent the oldest vampire, and I represent the combination of the two." She puts her hand on her stomach. "This child represents our future."

Topher's eyes grow at least two sizes. "What child, Amelia? Are you...Are you pregnant?"

She nods. "I don't need a test to tell me. I've had the suspicion for a while now."

Topher places a hand on her stomach. "Oh, my God. I never thought this could happen."

"Me neither," she answers. Amelia turns to me. "This child needs you to help in any way you can. Pave the way for him and what his future holds."

"Okay," I whisper. Amelia clasps her fingers through mine again, and we follow Topher inside the unassuming building. I don't know what I expected, but this isn't it. The room is huge and full of at least two hundred lycan. Where'd they park?

"Where's Jasper?"

"He's in the back. I'll let him know you're here." Topher leaves the two of us standing not far from the front door.

"Are you sure about this?" I ask.

"Nope," she answers, pulling me toward the crowd. As we pass, most of the lycan ignore us, while some snarl and even growl.

Whispers of "bloodsucker" and "vamp" can be heard throughout the room as we make our way to the front.

"Celeste!" Leann appears out of nowhere and wraps her arms around my shoulders. "I'm so glad you could make it."

"You look hot," Alex says, stepping out from behind his mother.

"Thank you?" I answer, not sure what the correct response to that statement is.

"Alex, that's not appropriate," Samantha chastises her brother. "She's a bloodsucker. You don't have to talk to her."

"Hi Samantha," I say with a wave. "You look nice."

"Whatever." She turns, leaving the four of us standing alone.

"I'm sorry about that. She's not taking Xavier's death well. None of us is, to be honest. She's just handling it her way." Leann turns toward the small stage in front. "The initiation is about to begin."

Topher is the first to appear from behind a thick red curtain. The lycan erupt with howls and applause as he walks to the center of the stage. "Good evening, my brothers and sisters. We've gathered here tonight to celebrate the turning of a new Alpha." The crowd erupts again.

"This feels like a dream," I whisper for Amelia's ears only.

"Agreed," she answers through our connection.

Jasper walks on stage, and in the few days since I've seen him, he seems bigger. His muscles are more defined, and his normally clean-shaven face is covered in a beard. "What the hell? What happened to him?"

"Alpha," Amelia answers. "Something happens genetically when they become Alpha. They must be the strongest. His body transformed to show that."

Jasper smiles and waves to his audience. "It is my honor to represent you as the next Alpha of North Mississippi. My father was honest, fair, and true. As your Alpha, I pledge to do the same." Howls can be heard throughout the room. "I will fight for the lycan and our traditions."

"What about the bloodsuckers?" someone in the back yells.

Jasper takes a deep breath. "I have no quarrels with

vampires. As far as I'm concerned, we will work together as one team."

Some of the lycan cheer, while some stay quiet. "We don't want to be a team with them," my friend from the back yells through the crowd.

"Then you will need to find another pack to join." Jasper doesn't back down. "As long as I am your leader, we will not fight our friends."

"Friends? Are you stupid, boy?"

Jasper explodes into wolf form. The once small black wolf is at least twice the size I remember and terrifying.

"Amelia, do something."

"No. Jasper has to do this on his own," she answers. "If we interfere, it will only strengthen the rebellion."

Jasper is on top of the man who shifted into a small brown wolf. In an instant, he rips the throat out of the brown wolf, throwing it across the room. He turns, facing his new pack. Each one lowers to their knees, bowing their heads in submission.

"He's now their Alpha, and they will follow him wherever he leads." Amelia bows her head toward Jasper, leaving me not sure what to do.

"It's time for the mating bond," a woman announces from the front of the room. All unbonded women between the ages of eighteen and twenty-one are required to participate in the ceremony.

"*Oh, hell no,*" I say for Amelia only. I turn back to see Jasper transformed back into human form and walking toward the front. He's wearing a pair of sweatpants that have appeared out of nowhere.

A group of at least twenty women lines the front of the stage. "You know how this works," the woman continues. "Our Alpha will choose his mate from the selection on stage, and the two will be bonded for life." The crowd begins howling their cheers.

I can't stop the tears from forming in my eyes. I close them, hoping to hide the pain. Each girl on stage is beautiful in their own right and are lycan. I can't compete with that. The room that was full of noise moments ago suddenly goes still. I refuse to open my eyes, not wanting to be a part of whatever is happening.

"Celeste, open your eyes," a deep voice says next to me.

"No." I shake my head. "I can't watch."

A large hand slides onto my cheek, turning my face. "Open your eyes, my mate. I choose you, Celeste Luquire. I choose you."

"God, this feels familiar," Amelia says as Topher comes to her side.

new beginnings

FOLLOWING JASPER'S MATE CHOICE, the rest of the ceremony is relatively boring. The lycan form a line, each congratulating both of us. To my surprise, most of the lycan are friendly and shake my hand or give me a slight hug. Jasper has kept his hand on me the entire time, and I'm grateful. As the last of the line makes its way through the impromptu receiving line, I turn toward my newly named mate, taking in his new appearance.

"Why are you staring at me?" he asks, giving me a side-eye.

"You look different," I answer with a smile.

"Good different or bad different?"

I nudge him with my elbow. "The jury's still out," I lie. He looks hot, and it's taking every bit of my strength not to wrap myself around him.

He squeezes my elbow as the last person moves in

front of us. Leann wraps her arms around me, pulling me close. "I'm so glad it was you." She pulls back, wiping a tear. "You make him happy. Welcome to the family, Celeste."

"Thank you, Mrs. Daniels."

"Call me Leann, please."

"Thank you, Leann."

"You did good, bro," Alex says, moving behind his mother. "Have fun tonight." He wiggles his eyebrows at his older brother. "If you know what I mean…"

"Alex, that's enough," Leann scolds. "Good night." She bows her head to her son.

"Good night, Mom. I love you."

"That's everyone," Topher says, clasping his hands behind him. "You did well, Jasper."

Jasper bows his head to Topher. "Thank you."

Amelia joins her husband and offers her congratulations. "Celeste, I'm not feeling great. Do you mind if we go?"

"No, of course not. I'll find a ride."

She smiles, knowingly before hugging me. *"Be safe,"* she whispers through my mind.

"Now who's being the mom?" I smirk with my words.

I watch the two of them leave and the building nearly clear out before turning toward my mate. "So, do you plan on telling me what this mate thing means?"

Jasper turns toward me, lifting our joined hands to his lips. "It means I'm yours if you'll have me."

Butterflies take flight. "I'll have to think about it."

"While you're thinking, want to get out of here?"

"I'd love to." We walk hand in hand through the front door and to his antique truck. "Do I get to drive?"

"I was just made Alpha. It's too early for Alex to take over, so no. I'm driving." He laughs with his answer.

I punch his shoulder. "Jerk. If my driving is bad, you can blame my teacher." I slide into the door he holds open for me. "He wasn't the best."

"I'm not going to argue with you on that. He was highly distracted by you and probably didn't do the best job he could have."

He's behind the steering wheel in an instant, and the truck roars to life. I have no idea where we're going, nor do I care. He turns onto a familiar dirt road and toward the lake where he took me on our first driving lesson. The nearly full moon glistens off the lake below, setting the perfect scene.

"This is beautiful." Jasper pulls the truck to a stop not far from where we parked last time.

"Give me a minute." He slides out of his side, pulling down the tailgate, and jumps in the back, doing something I can't see. My door is pulled open, and Jasper is standing beside the door seconds later. "My lady," he says, holding his hand toward me.

Jasper leads me to the bed of the truck and lifts me inside like I weigh nothing. "I brought a blanket if you get cold."

"I'm a vampire...we don't really get hot or cold."

"Yeah, I didn't think about that." He spreads the blanket out behind us, turning it into a makeshift bed.

"The stars are beautiful tonight," I say awkwardly. Truthfully, I don't know what's about to happen, and my stomach feels like an entire family of butterflies are taking flight. I lay back on the blanket, looking at the shiny dots above.

He jumps up beside me, lying next to me. "What are we doing, Jasper?"

He points to a cluster of stars directly over our heads. "Do you see those three stars, bunched together?"

"Orion's belt?"

He turns his head toward me. "I should've known I couldn't impress you with my Googled knowledge of astronomy." He laughs.

"You don't have to impress me."

"But I want to."

I turn my head to face him. "Jasper Daniels, I've been impressed by you since the first night we met. You don't have to do anything special for that to continue."

"You amaze me, Celeste Luquire. I don't think you know how wonderful you are." I resist the urge to look down at his words.

"No, but I'm not opposed to you telling me every once in a while." I move at vampire speed and straddle his hips with mine. Grabbing a wrist in each hand, I hold them tight to his sides. "I'm not letting you go, ever."

"Good," he answers. Our lips crash together, and we spend the rest of the night exploring each other in every way possible.

Eight Months Later

"Celeste, I swear. If this baby waits too much longer, I'm not going to be able to walk." Amelia waddles into the living room of the Mandeville home. "I'm only five feet tall, for goodness' sake. If he keeps growing, he's going to come out bigger than me."

"He's the son of the lycan Alpha and a lycan-vampire hybrid. He can be as big as he wants to be."

"That's what I'm afraid of." She laughs. "I'm going to have two of them trying to boss me around."

The swinging door opens as Topher enters the room. "No matter how hard you try and convince people otherwise, anyone who's met you for longer than five minutes knows you are always the boss."

"Amen," I whisper.

"I heard that," Amelia retorts.

"There are three weeks left before his due date. You can make it." I offer comfort from across the room.

She leans back, blowing air from her lips. "I know. I'm just enjoying complaining."

"Have you heard from Jasper?" Topher asks, grabbing one of Amelia's feet and rubbing gently. The moan that leaves her mouth is embarrassing, even for me.

"He texted this morning. Everything seems to be going well. I'll go back up there after the baby comes," I answer. "I'm anxious to meet my brother. Have you decided on a name yet?"

The two of them share a look. "You'll have to wait until he decides to make his appearance," Amelia adds.

"I wish you were having him in the hospital. I'm worried about my brother being born in a bathtub."

"Considering we don't have any idea what he's going to *do* after birth, I think a home birth is the safest for everyone." Topher switches out Amelia's feet, rubbing the other one.

"He could pop out and eat everyone," Amelia says with a smile.

"Are you talking about those movies you made me watch?"

"Don't mock the Twilight series," Topher interjects. "Those movies helped me fall in love with Amelia."

"I thought it was my boobs?"

Topher laughs. "Those helped."

"Ouch." Amelia places a hand on her stomach. "Your son is trying to kick me to death." She clinches again. "Oh," she sighs. "That felt different." She slides to the front of her chair, and a gush of water hits the floor. "Was that...did my water just break?"

"What do we do?" Topher stands with a look of

panic on his face. "Do I get Fran? Fran!" he screams into the house.

I stand, taking control. "Topher, go get the water ready and make sure the temperature is set correctly."

Fran rushes into the room. "What's going on?" She looks around for the emergency. "Who spilled water on the floor?" Her eyes grow several sizes as the realization of the situation sinks in. "Oh, my. Amelia? Are you in labor?"

"I think so," she scrunches her face in pain. "Either that or he really is eating me from the inside out."

"Topher, go." He runs upstairs at my words. "Amelia, can you walk?" I move in front of her, helping her to her feet. While she's been pregnant, I've read every medical book I can get my hands on about home births and beyond. I'm prepared for anything from a natural, easy birth to a C-section.

She stands, wrapping one arm around Fran's shoulders and one around mine. "I'm good. Let's get in that tub. I don't think he's taking it slow." We inch our way up the stairs, finding Topher staring at an empty tub.

"Where's the water?"

"I...I forgot how to turn it on."

Amelia laughs. "Why are you the one with pregnancy brain? I'm the one about to push a watermelon out of my vagina."

"Move, boy," Fran pushes Topher out of the way and starts the water running. She turns on the heater we purchased and fills the tub to the line.

"I'm sorry," Topher announces from the corner of the bathroom.

Amelia slides into the tub, pulling off her wet clothes in the process. "It's fine. Come hold my hand. I may or may not break every bone in it during this birth. It's the payment you receive for putting this huge thing inside of me."

"I can do that." Topher moves to the side of the tub, grabbing her hand. "Amelia, we're going to be parents. I don't think it's hit me until now."

"We are." She smiles. Her face contorts to one of pain and confusion. "We're going to become parents now. He's coming! Celeste, what do I do?"

"Can I check your cervix?"

Amelia's breathing hard, practicing the techniques we worked on together. "I don't care what you do. Get him out."

I do a quick check, finding her ready to push. "It's time. Push." Less than two minutes later, a head full of bright red hair appears at the bottom of the tub. "His head is out. Keep pushing." I gently help his shoulders enter this world, keeping his body in the correct position. The moment he's out, I lift him above the water, clearing his nose and mouth, and the sounds of tiny howls mixed with cries echo off the bathroom walls.

Topher immediately starts crying. "Look what we did, Amelia."

I cut the cord, making sure to follow the sequence I've practiced hundreds of times. "Congratulations, he's beautiful." I hand the large baby to his mother, wiping the tears from my eyes. "Welcome to the world, little brother."

"Yes. Welcome, Edon Viktor St. James," Amelia says, holding him tightly to her chest. "You're even more beautiful than I thought you'd be."

"You named him after your father and mine?"

Topher smiles, wrapping his arms around his family. "We named him after two of the strongest men we've ever known."

Tears fill my eyes. "Thank you both. Viktor would be proud."

"You really think Viktor would be proud of a vampire-wolf hybrid baby bearing his name?" Amelia says, laughing.

"If you put it that way, probably not." I reach for baby Edon. "Fran can clean him up while we get you cleaned up."

An hour later, Amelia is in the middle of a king-sized bed and looks smaller than life without the baby in her stomach. Topher is next to her, holding a burrito-wrapped Edon. After Fran cleaned him up, his hair is even brighter red than I originally thought.

"I can't get over all this hair," Topher says, rubbing the small curls between his fingers. "He looks like he has a mortgage and three kids."

"That's not funny." Amelia swats his leg. "Thank you, Celeste. Thank you for everything."

Leaving the room, I shut the door behind me, giving

them the time they need as a family. My phone buzzes the moment the door closes.

How's my favorite vampire?

Missing you, wolf.

Good, come home.

I smile, thinking of Jasper as my home.

epilogue

"TELL me again why we chose to come back to Ravenwood?" Emeryn says, jumping behind the wheel of her Porsche.

"Because you need a degree, and I enjoy the interactions." I slide into the passenger seat and prepare to hold on for dear life as she flies around the curves that lead to campus. "However, I'm going to have to start driving. Your driving scares the shit out of me."

"Whatever. You know you love the cheap thrill it provides. Hell, we need some sort of thrill. Sitting in a classroom all day doesn't provide many. I mean, why can't one of the professors be hot?" She turns toward me. "Oh, maybe Ollie could come back for a semester. At least he's easy on the eyes."

"He's too old for you, plus, he has vampire things to do."

"*We* have vampire things to do," she retorts. Emeryn pulls the car to a stop in the parking lot, and we walk toward the main building. "So, how are things with that wolf of yours?"

"They're good. Actually, they're great." I can't hide the smile on my face.

"Uh, huh. I see that smirk. I've decided I'm not ready to settle down. The way I see it, I have hundreds of years to find the right one. Who knows what the future holds?" She holds the door open as I enter.

"You've got your whole life ahead of you and countless men to meet."

Emeryn smiles. "Oh, I plan to do more than *meet* them."

"Hi, Celeste," Stephanie says, passing by the two of us. "Emeryn." She turns her nose up as she passes my former roommate.

"I don't think she likes me," Emeryn announces, heading upstairs to our first class.

"She's not sure what she feels. Compulsion does that to people sometimes. She knows something is strange with us but doesn't understand what. Part of her may associate you with a strange feeling."

"You're the one who performed the compulsion on her. Why's she pissed at me?" Emeryn huffs a laugh.

"Maybe because she can tell you're a bitch." I laugh as she swats me on the butt.

Our three shared classes pass quickly. Butterflies

take flight when we exit the main building, and I see a familiar truck. Since becoming Alpha, Jasper's updated his transportation to a truck that's only three years old instead of twenty.

I can't hide the smile on my face when I see him leaning against the door. His arms are crossed over his chest, and his long legs are crossed at the ankles. He looks sexy as hell. The full beard he magically grew before becoming Alpha has filled in more, and he's even taller than he was a year ago.

"Hey, dog," I tease, stepping in front of him.

"Woof," he answers with a deep smile.

"You're a sight for sore eyes." I stretch on my toes, kissing him on the lips and lingering longer than necessary.

"Jasper," Emeryn greets the Alpha of North Mississippi.

"Emeryn," he responds.

She's not overly fond of Jasper, and no one blames her since his brother was the one who started this whole mess. "I'll see you back at the house, Celeste. Can your wolf take you home?"

"I think I can work that out," he answers.

"Keep it under eighty," I yell toward Emeryn as she walks away. She responds with a one-finger wave before disappearing into the parking lot.

"How's she adjusting?" Jasper opens my door, ushering me inside.

"Remarkably well. She's planning out her ho years already."

Jasper's laugh fills the truck cab as we pull off campus. Ten minutes later, we turn into the familiar lake that has become our "spot."

"What the hell?" Anger fills Jasper's voice as he pulls in behind a bulldozer and a large pile of trees and debris. "Did someone buy this land from old man Elkins?" He's out of the truck, heading straight for the only man in sight.

"Hey!" he shouts, moving quickly. "What the hell are you doing?"

The man turns, facing the giant, moving quickly toward him. "Clearing off the land for the new owner."

"New owner?" He turns toward me. "Dammit. Who bought the land?"

"I'm not sure, sir. All I know is there are plans for a house to be built not far from the water's edge. The owner has the plans already and specified which trees are to be cleared." He moves quickly toward his truck and leaves before Jasper completely loses his cool.

Jasper runs his hands through his messy hair. "I always thought I'd somehow be the one to buy this land. I guess it wasn't in the cards."

I pull my backpack off and slide a large roll from inside. "Speaking of that, can you take a look at these for me?"

"Yeah," his voice sounds defeated. "What is it?"

"They're blueprints for a class I'm taking this semester. I have no history with blueprint design. I thought maybe you could check over my work."

"Sure." He carries them back to the hood of the truck, rolling them out smoothly. "Did you do these?"

"I did," I lie.

"I'm no expert, but they look good to me." He points to the lake off to the side and the log cabin not far from it. "This is beautiful. Maybe one day you can draw the plans for our house." He moves in front of me, wrapping his arms around my waist.

"I'm glad you like them. They're the plans for our new cabin that's being built on this land." I pull back, looking him in the eyes. "Old man Elkins sold his land to me for a very fair compensation. He's going to be retiring to a tropical island where he can drink fruity drinks all day and behave badly all night."

Jasper wrinkles his forehead. "What are you saying?"

"I'm saying, this land is ours, and the plans on the hood of your truck are of the home that is being built on it."

"Celeste? When did you do this?"

I shrug. "My classes were boring."

He pulls me close. "I love you, Celeste Luquire."

"I love you, Jasper Daniels."

. . .

For more Vampires of New Orleans, check out "Garden of Rage and Ruin." Violet's story is both heartbreaking and charming, and the perfect addition to the New Orleans Vampires.

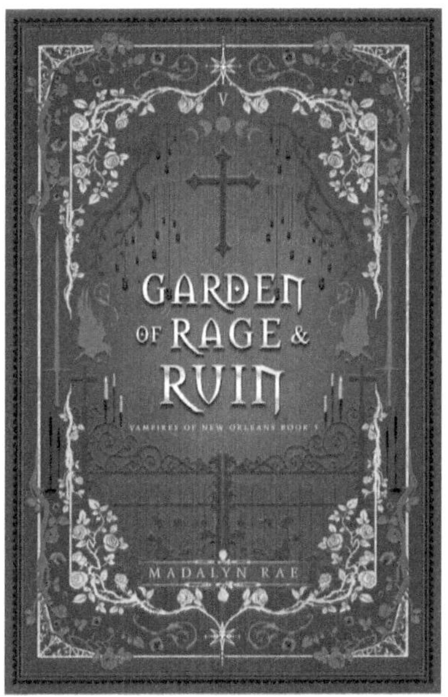

If you enjoyed Celeste's story, please consider leaving a review on the "Zon." Your reviews help me rise in the ranks. Thank you!

about the author

Madalyn Rae is the pen name for an author who loves telling a story. As a teacher of tiny humans during the day and author by night, she hopes she's able to draw you into her world of fantasy, make-believe, and love, even for a brief moment.

She lives on the Gulf Coast's beautiful white, sandy beaches, with her two loyal yet mildly obnoxious dogs, Whiskey and Tippi. She's the mother of two amazing adult children, a son-in-law, and a beautiful new grandson.

When not teaching or pretending to write, Madalyn is immersed in the world of music. Whether playing an instrument or singing a song, she is privileged to know that music is the true magic of the universe.

The Magical Midlife Series

Season of Bone and Blood-Book 1

Season of Storm and Ash-Book 2

Vampires of New Orleans Series

Garden of the Past-Prequel Novella

Garden of Secret and Shadow-Book 1

Garden of Mystery and Intrigue -Book 2

Garden of Discovery and Love- Book 3

Ravenwood-Spin off

Garden of Rage and Ruin-Book 5

Vmapires of Charleston

Voyage of Death and Desire-Book 1

Voyage of Fury and Fate-Book 2

Voyage of Magic and Malice-Book 3

The Elementals Series

Birth of the Phoenix-Adria's Novella-Prequel

Phoenix of the Sea- Elementals Book 1

Guardian of the Sea- Murphy's Novella

Ashes of the Wind-Elementals Book 2

Embers of the Flame-Keegan's Novella

Fire of the Sky-Elementals Book 3

Morally Gray Novella Series

Full Moon Christmas

Nipping at Your Nose

Fallen

Lucky